Co

FROM PAGE 384 OF

THE SURGEON'S HANDBOOK ON THE TREATMENT OF WOUNDED IN WAR:
A PRIZE ESSAY (1884)

AUTHOR: FRIEDRICH VON ESMARCH (1823-1908)

PUBLISHER: SAMPSON, LOW, MARSTON, SEARLE, AND RIVINGTON - LONDON

OPERATIONS WITH ARTIFICIAL LIGHT

1. IN WAR THE SURGEON HAS FREQUENTLY TO OPERATE AT NIGHT; AND ONBOARD SHIP DURING AN ENGAGEMENT THE NECESSARY OPERATIONS MUST ACCORDING TO THE RULES BE PERFORMED WITH ARTIFICIAL LIGHT BELOW DECK.

2. FOR MOST OPERATIONS A STRONG LIGHT UPON THE SEAT OF OPERATION IS ABSOLUTELY NECESSARY; AND THE SURGEON MUST KNOW WHAT TO DO, IF, AS COMMONLY HAPPENS, THE PLACE ITSELF IS ONLY INSUFFICIENTLY LIGHTED.

3. THE WAX-TORCH IS A SIMPLE AND VERY GOOD MEANS OF OBTAINING LIGHT: IT IS MADE OUT OF THE COMMON WAX-TAPER, ABOUT THE THICKNESS OF A QUILL, THREE OR FOUR OF WHICH ARE TWISTED TOGETHER LIKE A ROPE. TO PROTECT THE HAND AGAINST THE HOT WAX AS IT TRICKLES DOWN, THE TORCH IS PLACED THROUGH A DISK OF PASTE BOARD, WHICH HAS A HOLE CUT IN ITS CENTRE.

THIS BOOK HAS BEEN TYPESET IN OLD STANDARD TT - DESIGNED BY
ALEXEY KRYUKOV

THE OLD STANDARD FONT FAMILY IS AN ATTEMPT TO REVIVE A SPECIFIC TYPE OF MODERN (CLASSICIST) STYLE OF SERIF TYPEFACES, VERY COMMONLY USED IN VARIOUS EDITIONS PRINTED IN THE LATE 19TH AND EARLY 20TH CENTURY, BUT ALMOST COMPLETELY ABANDONED LATER.

How to be Happy

Not a Self-Help Book. Seriously.

Old and New, Common and Rare
Stories, Prose, and Poems

by

Iain S. Thomas

central avenue
publishing
2015

www.centralavenuepublishing.com

Published in Canada. Printed in the United States of America.

First print edition published by Central Avenue Publishing,
an imprint of Central Avenue Marketing Ltd.

HOW TO BE HAPPY

ISBN 978-1-77168-031-8 (pbk)
ISBN 978-1-77168-032-5 (ebk)

10 9 8 7 6 5 4 3

1. POETRY / Subjects & Themes   2. PHILOSOPHY / General

Cover Design: Michelle Halket

For my wife for being both the woman I love and the woman I need; for my mother for her tireless spirit; for my late father for his wisdom and bad jokes; for anyone who's ever shared their time with me and read what I write; and finally, for Michelle, my tireless publisher for her constant support.

But not for Sandra.

Although I do hope she's finally getting help, wherever she is.

HOW TO BE HAPPY

Iain S. Thomas @IWroteThisForU - Jan 1
One day, if you're lucky, you'll say something beautiful and
true and people will love you for a little while.

To: Iain S. Thomas
From: Sandra J.
re: NEW BOOK!

Hey Iain!

Glad you had a nice break. The idea sounds great, I am looking forward to seeing what you've already written and getting it out there. Self-help market is huge! Good route. Maybe put something spiritual in it?

For example, did you read the thing about the young boy who wrote about going to heaven and made millions?

Do a good job on this and it could be great. Make it something uplifting – Lord knows even I need that right about now what with all my Christmas bills coming in – LOL! Chicken Soup for the Soul kind of thing. I hate to say this, but sad people seem to find you inspiring. Might be another way to tap that market. $$

I know you're aware that all these other books like your first one are out there now. You know, the 'kind-of-free-verse-poems' to some unnamed lost love that's never really specified. I get a few "unwritten letters to the one I love" books pitched to me every week.

Soooo, what I'm trying to say is that your previous stuff isn't as original as it was back in 2007. Going in a new direction will be a good thing!

Let's put a pin on the board and aim for release in December, in time for Christmas. You do your genius thing and don't worry, I'll set everything in motion here.

Kind regards, Sandra

Iain S. Thomas @IWroteThisForU · Jan 11
Everyone just kind of leans their expectations of who you are
on you and it makes you petrified of who you really might be.

To: Sandra J.
From: Iain S. Thomas
re: NEW BOOK!

Hi Sandra,

I'm glad you think this is a good idea, but I'm not sure we're on the same page. I just want to make something that means something to me and to others, not a self-help book. Does that make sense?

Yes, I have been kicking something around for a while, like I said on the conference call, but I'm not sure it aligns with what you're saying.

I'm also not sure that the people who read my work should be described as sad. Sometimes they're sad and sometimes they're not.

I'd like to meet in the middle if we can?

But, let's not call it a self-help book, it just feels cheap. I'm not going to pretend I've got all the answers. No one's got all the answers. I have trouble calling myself a writer, let alone a poet, most days and people who claim to be gurus or prophets or whatever don't sit well with me.

I don't trust them.

We're all alone out here in the dark, all I want to do is try to set something on fire so we can see where we are.

I don't want to pretend I've got the map.

That might sound harsh. I am looking forward to doing this, I just want it to be useful, like it actually does something. I think if it makes you feel inspired for an hour and then you forget about it, then it's useless and we've failed.

Regardless of all that, I think writing it will be good. For me especially. Maybe other people too if we're lucky.

I've attached what I've already written.

I've also attached a short story I wrote about an insane museum curator who fantasises about writing a science fiction movie. I'm just experimenting. Not sure where it's going or if it's going anywhere but I'm sending it to you so you can let me know if you see anything in it. Just humour me?

Keep well, Iain

How To Be Happy!

Firstly, understand that you should be happy and if you're unhappy for a long time, that's not natural.

The majority of the human race isn't always unhappy and just pretending to make it by. I mean, sure, everyone's struggling and we are all "fighting a great battle," as someone smarter than me once said, but we're supposed to be happy.

Secondly, drink more water. There's a very good chance, or at least I read in a study somewhere, that if you're depressed it could be because you're dehydrated, so the solution could be as simple as that. If you want to go and get a glass of water right now before you carry on reading, you can do that.

Thirdly, you probably need to exercise. If you don't exercise, you don't have energy and energy is what lets you do stuff which makes you happy. Besides, it's hard to be happy if you feel unhealthy.

If you smoke, it's hard to always have that voice at the back of your head going, "You should quit smoking, you should quit smoking, you should quit smoking ... come on," because then you end up spending all your mental energy on that instead of devoting it to doing stuff that makes you happy. There's only so much space in your head, leave some of it open for being happy.

Note: I have brought up either "to do stuff" or "doing stuff" to make you happy because "stuff" itself can't make you happy, only "doing stuff" will make you happy.

Don't sit on the couch while someone vacuums around you, feeling horrible about the fact that you can't move because you're too depressed. Don't feel like a ghost, like the memory of someone who used to look like you but now doesn't know exactly who they are.

Get up.

Don't feel like a feather, drifting out of control on someone else's breath. Although if you think of yourself as a feather or believe that feeling like a feather could be a good thing, then that's cool, go with that. Maybe go skydiving?

There is no pressure to become who "you" are at a specific point in your life, you are who "you" are, you do not become "you" one day in the future, you are always you, with everything you do.

Do not sacrifice the person you are today for the person you could be tomorrow.

There's only ever now.

You should still save money because otherwise you'll be poor one day and that very rarely makes anyone happy. Unless the person in question, being you in this case, was someone with too much money, who neglected the people around them who loved them, and then only found out what love is after they'd lost everything.

Which is the plot for a whole bunch of movies.

And maybe movies and stories are nearly always clichés but we still relate to them because we like to believe our life is a story. Because all stories, at least most of them, have a happy ending. But we need to be happy, now, before we end.

I worry that most of us feel like we're always in the middle of the story and that it's too easy to think, while you're there, that there's no other way to feel. How can you ever really feel "I've done it!" and think that it's the end. Because after you write "They lived happily ever after," the typewriter has to carry on, the words have to keep going. You have to do the work of living.

"Then they went for ice-cream. Then they had a fight about what to watch on TV. Then they had makeup sex. Then they didn't talk over breakfast. Then they fell in love again. Then they hated each other. Then one of them went for a drive and nearly died in a car crash and they loved each other again. Then one of them slipped in the kitchen, at the Welcome-Home-From-The-Hospital party, on a small puddle of water near the refrigerator, and hit their head on the corner of the counter, and they died. Then the other person was left alone with nothing but empty words of comfort from family and friends and their grief. In truth, they only lived happily ever after for several years, until one of them died."

Time doesn't pause in some eternal moment of bliss, sheared sideways like that candy that has writing all the way through, as much as we'd like it to. As much as we'd wish it to. There's a moment after the end, and then another, and then another, and then another and you have to actually live through those moments. And sometimes, for some of us maybe, sometimes that means you have to be strong. Because the individual moments of nearly anything can be difficult.

I'm getting distracted, sorry. I honestly thought writing this book would make me happy. I thought helping you, whoever you are, would help me. Maybe it isn't. Let me carry on and we'll talk about how it's going later.

Don't buy an expensive car. You will always worry about scratching it, and you will scratch it, because scratching and damaging something you love is just human.

I don't mean to dump all of this on you like a set of rules for life. Life isn't a board game. Life is a series of events that you have the chance to influence. You are present at these events. You are aware of them.

You're still alive when you're asleep, even if you aren't really present and aware, but I've never been able to be around myself while that's happening to really check. You're alive in your dreams. Someone has to be experiencing all that stuff, right? Depending on which dream we're talking about. Everyone has that one where you're not wearing any pants at school and everyone's laughing at you and you don't know why until you look down and BAM! You're naked. And the other one where you're trying to fight back against something but your punches are so slow that it doesn't really feel like you're doing anything, like your punches aren't having any real effect. Or when you try to scream, and nothing comes out.

I guess that's a feeling of hopelessness or helplessness. I actually just meant to write 'helplessness' there but I'm not going to delete the word, 'hopelessness'.

Sorry. I'm trying not to delete things. Maybe deleting the things you don't need makes you happy. But sometimes deleting things is the easy way out.

My intention isn't to bring you down.

If you're reading this then maybe you're already down and now all I'm doing is bringing you even lower because I've started writing a whole bunch of these things but if I look at them, they all seem very obvious. Like you could find some of them in one of those magazines that tells you to be happy with who you are but also, here's how you really should be having sex and here's some diet tips. Because you're fat.

Now I'm kind of sorry I started down this road at all because no doubt by now you're probably thinking that actually, this isn't a very happy book at all. It's kind of terrifying to be me right now because what if you feel cheated and you hate me? I'm really, really sorry if that's happened.

Wait! I've got another one:

Don't do jobs you don't enjoy unless you either need or really, really want the money. If just having money makes you happy and if a job you hate gives you that, that's your decision and we all have to respect it. But we do all worry about and love you. Just so you know. Even if, sometimes, you find it hard to love yourself.

Don't buy into irony or cynicism as a lifestyle. It's not a lifestyle, it's shit pretending to be a lifestyle - how can you be happy if you spend all your time dismissing things? People pigeonhole other people all the time so if people start calling you that "cynical and ironic person" then you need to watch out because it's hard to ever change that. I've moved cities and countries because of who people thought I was. So that I could find somewhere where I could be someone new.

You shouldn't care about what other people think of you because you should control your own happiness. But not caring about other people has its own set of problems that'll mess you up in the long run if you're not careful.

There was a research article I read with the headline, "Love Is A Single Act Committed By Two Brains," because of the way oxytocin levels rose in a mother and a son when they hugged. I wish more poets became scientists because then there would be more headlines that read, "Love Is A Single Act Committed By Two Hearts." Which is a much better headline, in my opinion. Does the part of your body where you experience being happy really matter? Only poets and scientists would disagree.

But scientists are scientists and poets are poets and maybe they're the same thing on different days of the week.

I have no idea how we got here.

I'm sure if you were a kind person you would say, "Don't be sorry," but you've paid for this book and now the person writing it is kind of collapsing and going off on strange tangents and there's not even a hint of actual help yet, real, actual help, and things really just seem to be going from bad to worse because it sounds like the person writing it is actually just listing off a series of mistakes they've made - and - AND they really don't seem like they're in any kind of position to be offering advice on happiness.

I really am trying here, give me a break! Sorry, I don't mean to sound defensive. All this self-awareness is making it impossible to actually get into this.

I can't get anything right.

Don't think that.

The last few sentences are an example of a thought process not to start, ok?

Ok.

Be like a dog. I've read that somewhere before. Dogs are almost always happy and when they're sad, it's usually because their owner has gone away or they think someone is taking a walk without them but then when they see you again, they're happy. And they forget they were ever sad because they're permanently in the now.

Someone's throwing a ball, right now. There's food in my bowl, now. I'm sleeping in the sun, now. It's always now and it's great. That's dogs.

I don't think it's as easy for people to forget to be sad. I think people sometimes don't even stop being sad when the thing that was making them sad stops being there.

We're all just too good at remembering. Not phone numbers or addresses or anything, those are easy to forget; but how you feel. How you feel is always there, just below the surface. Like a tattoo on your soul.

Maybe it's a name. Maybe it's a picture. Maybe it's a date. Maybe it's line after line after line of the things you think to yourself before you sleep.

Don't ever look at a swimming pool and think, "The leaf is nature's cigarette butt." That's horrible and just because the pool is full of leaves doesn't give you the right to completely dismiss the Divine Phenomenon that is nature. The universe is nature breathing.

Nature is one of those things that can make you happy. It's part of the stuff that you can do that'll make you happy.

Nature's made me happy before, I remember being happy in nature before.

It's not like I spend a lot of time outdoors so maybe I'm not the best person to talk to about this. I don't think I've ever walked into a crowded room full of people and yelled, "Hey! Let's go for a hike!"

I once walked into a crowded room and yelled, "Hey! Let's play some video games!"

You need to watch out for that too because the things you do in video games aren't real. If you kill a dragon in a video game, in real life you've just wasted a few hours of time. You haven't actually learned anything, like how to kill an actual dragon, which perhaps isn't the constant threat I was led to believe as a child.

But then, reading about killing a dragon isn't that much better and what's wrong with reading or just enjoying the relatively limited time you have here? We're all here for such a short amount of time, shouldn't we spend it being happy? Being good to each other, and ourselves?

I don't know. I might be wrong about the video games.

Wear your watch on a different wrist each day and if you forget to do it, then just tell people you do it and when they ask why, tell them, "Because it means that I never get used to checking a specific wrist for the time, and thus, it makes my brain more agile, so I'm better prepared for the unexpected."

And then people will think you're very wise and deep and interesting because of what you're doing, and because you used the word "thus" in a sentence, and you'll feel loved for a little while, even though it isn't really true and you keep your watch on the same wrist every day.

Wear clothes that fit you. Seriously. Everyone always misses this but you know that scene in the movie where the girl or the guy that was the ugly duckling suddenly becomes incredibly beautiful? They just did their hair up nicely and put on clothes that fit them. Ugly ducklings don't have the luxury of high fashion but you do, and you should take advantage of it as much as you can.

You will look at yourself and think, "Yeah, I like this."

You'll pose in front of the mirror and try to look off into the distance while trying to look at yourself, so your eyes will do this weird back-and-forth thing, trying to trick the speed of light. You can't ever look at yourself when you're trying to look away.

Whenever you're looking at your eyes in the mirror, you have to be staring right into them and you need to watch out for that because it's easy to disappear inside yourself, to find blemishes, pimples, wrinkles, imperfections, all the things that make you think, "Who is this person and why are they me?"

The more you look in a mirror, the unhappier you'll be.

Never find yourself in a situation where you have to hold and comfort the person that's just been hurt, and you're the one who just hurt them. It'll feel like your arms are covered in spikes and you're hurting and killing the thing you love, just by holding and comforting it.

Holding someone you love and who loves you will make you happy. It's not the only thing that'll make you happy but it is one of the bigger ones.

Holding someone who makes you feel lonely doesn't do that. Don't do that.

There are real assholes out there, assholes who'll take your time and your money and your love but they're not the whole world. They're just a few assholes.

Don't walk out on the world.

The world is filled with beautiful, smart, wonderful people and if you walk out on all of them then you're really only doing yourself a disservice. Stay with the world. It might not always feel like it, but the world has your back.

So does the universe. I like to believe that there was a grand, benevolent conspiracy on the part of everything to make you, you.

While that thought doesn't actually fix broken things, it sometimes makes me feel ok while I'm trying to fix them.

To be a part of the universe is human and to be human is to be happy. Or at least, to be human is to try to be happy.

I don't know.

I think you need to be ok with that, the not knowing everything bit. You don't have to be ok with your purchase though and if you feel like you've been ripped off, I'll understand. I've gotten over myself, honestly, you can tell me: I suck. Leave a bad review on Amazon and warn others, hopefully all the bad reviews will make sure that no one makes the mistake of buying this book again and then the people reading this now will be thinking, "Why is he doing all this apologising? We read the bad reviews, we know exactly what this is all about."

Here are some things you can try at home.

• Imagine you are the happiest you've ever been. Write down how that feels. Put it in your pocket and never lose that piece of paper, ever.

• Imagine someone really sad. Now imagine you're someone else, comforting them. Slowly start to pretend you are the person being comforted.

• Phone every person you've ever had a fight with, even if the fight was only ever in your head. Whisper the words, "I forgive you," when they pick up. Do not turn off caller ID.

• Draw every bad word you've ever called yourself on your body. Stand in the shower and pay attention to the way the words turn back into ink and disappear down the drain.

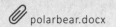

The Story Of An Insane Museum Curator And His Polar Bear

The light sabre arced through the air, incinerating molecules and atoms as it went. I somersaulted backwards, away from the harsh red glow of the dark lord's deadly weapon.

"No, no, no - that's a stupid story, no one would ever buy it. Maybe I should just stick to being a museum curator and give up on my dreams of writing a space opera. It's not a hard job, I see a museum, I curate it. I've curated hundreds in my time.

"Now if only I could do something about my neurosis that forces me to narrate my life out loud for everyone to hear," I said, to no one in particular.

"I think it'd be a wonderful story," said the stuffed polar bear in the corner.

"You're insane," I replied.

Iain S. Thomas @IWroteThisForU · Jan 13
There is no prose as inspiring as a single human being with
the courage to live well.

January 14, 2014

To: Iain S. Thomas
From: Sandra J.
re: NEW BOOK!

Iain,

Thank you for sending this. Let me first say, that I have the UTMOST respect for you and what you do - but, this really wasn't what we were looking for. There's *some* good bits in it (a few words here and there), so I've spoken to marketing about taking some of it and turning certain quotes into headlines for posters and banner ads and so on. Don't think you need me to tell you what the good bits are.

Our publishing company would have grave concerns about telling people not to buy the book or to leave bad reviews. It'd be the publishing equivalent of running a bath then deciding you want to make toast.

Play the game. (smiley face!) I know you are not really that person, but in this world, we all need to play it. Just delete the self-aware stuff and write it properly since currently it reads like some kind of literary performance art. Besides that one woman who gets naked all the time at MOMA, very few performance artists actually make any money.

Kind regards, Sandra

January 15, 2014

To: Sandra J.
From: Iain S. Thomas
re: NEW BOOK!

Hi Sandra,

I understand that there are things that need to be done in the marketing world or publishing or any business for that matter.

This book is different. I'm not trying to convince you of its merits – well maybe I am – I just want to make a book that means something to the person who reads it.

Thank you for your honest opinion, but this is how I see this book shaping up.

Still wondering what you thought about the insane museum curator short story?

Chat soon, Iain

Iain S. Thomas @IWroteThisForU - Jan 30
Sometimes I have a weird dream that we're all relatively brief
sparks of consciousness that live on a rock circling a ball of fire.

Iain S. Thomas @IWroteThisForU - Jan 30
And in the dream people get bored of this.

Iain S. Thomas @IWroteThisForU - Jan 30
Also, frustrated with petty, insignificant things.

Here at last, we shall be free.

The Moonlighter

In Uncategorized on January 31, 2014 at 5:30pm

Often, you'll wake up and say, "Fuck it. I don't want this job, this car, this life," and then get in your car, drive to your job and carry on living your life.

Not me.

I woke up one day and said that exact thing and actually meant it. I unplugged the landline, put my computer in the bath (and turned the tap on), then got stuck in the rum. Quite possibly the best day of my life really. I watched a lot of cat videos on my phone while I drank the rum. When I got bored of the videos, I went out and finished the rum on the pavement, watching the steel coffins whistle by. Some hooted angrily. More than a few looked pretty jealous and that made me smile because it struck me that most of them probably go to work, own their cars and live their lives in order to make other people jealous of them.

In other words, the basis of happiness in their lives is other people's unhappiness.

That thought in mind, I parked my car across the road, blocking the traffic, then pretended like it wasn't mine and went back inside the house. It got towed about 45 minutes later.

The rum finished, and, rip-roaring drunk and emotional, I stumbled inside and went to sleep on the couch. Later that night I got up, had a headache, drank lots of water, then went to bed.

The next morning I got up and, like any sensible adventurer, realised what a stupid, stupid thing I'd done. So I got out the classifieds section of the newspaper and started looking for work, bracing myself for the inevitable task of starting the whole process again, a job, a nice car, a better® life.

One ad struck me in some kind of particular way.

"Full-Time Moonlighter Required Urgently," read the headline.

Curious, and taking my second chance in twenty-four hours, I phoned the number at the bottom of the ad and waited while the phone droned peacefully in my ear.

"Hello?"

"Hello, I'm phoning about the ad."

"What ad?"

"The full-time moonlighter required ad. It's a joke isn't it?"

There was a brief awkward silence on the other end of the line followed by the distinctive sound of someone gesticulating silently at someone near them about something they'd done wrong earlier.

"No, no joke. We really do need you to start as soon as possible."

I figured one job was as good as another. And if it was a joke, it might be funny.

"Ok."

"Really?"

"Really."

We talked salary, which I won't talk about here because it's rude. But generally speaking, the figure was somewhere around hope and joy, happiness and somebody brushing pleasantly against you during a meal, in change.

We arranged to meet later on, after work, which made sense if it was a moonlighting position but I still didn't get how they could make it full time. The address was on the other side of town so I put on my suit and left early.

When I got there, there was a building that looked like an old bus depot, with cracked windows and a brown haze of dust covering everything. I was pretty sure this was the scene of the most elaborate, surreal mugging ever, when I saw a grubby-looking man in blue overalls with half an unlit cigarette hanging from his mouth. This would be a mugger, I assumed.

By the time I'd noticed him, he'd already started walking towards me and so I politely took out my wallet.

"I'm afraid the car's been towed but you can have this."

He looked at it thoughtfully for a second, shrugged, put it in his pocket and said, "Thanks. You're here about the job right?"

"Right. You're not a mugger are you?"

"Nope."

"I see. Could I have my wallet back?"

He scratched his neck, shrugged and then gave it back. He started walking away and even if he didn't ask me to follow him, I did.

"Are the offices nearby?"

"Offices?" he asked.

"Yes, the offices, I imagine the position I'm applying for, whatever it is, isn't here in the bus depot. Although considering the salary, I wouldn't really mind that much."

He grunted in that tired, couldn't-really-care kind of way that people in blue overalls with half-cigarettes hanging out of their mouths are very good at.

"I see," I said.

We soon came to a glowing red comet, melting the cement floor around it and destroying the gel in my hair, causing my get-a-job-haircut to look less than professional.

"Why is there a glowing red comet, melting the cement floor around it, sitting here?"

"This is the company car," said the man in the blue overalls.

"I see," I said, feeling my skin tan more and more by the second.

"Get on then."

Figuring this was as good a way to die as any, I stepped closer to the comet. The heat was quite unbearable and my clothes burst into flame but I carried on because it seemed like the polite thing to do.

After the first layer of flesh left me, I discovered that beneath my skin, a layer of silver had formed. I discovered I was featureless and shiny beneath my skin. I got onto the comet and it shot up, like a rocket, through the roof of the bus depot, with me on it, standing as still as one can stand on a round, glowing red comet travelling at the speed of, well, whatever speed a comet travels at.

It was after 5pm when I left and soon I arrived at my office, which was, of course, on the moon itself. There was a neatly folded package on the desk when I walked inside which explained pretty much the whole process. Apparently I was only responsible for lighting the moon over here. There are other people responsible for the other moons in the other parts of the world. It didn't seem like too much responsibility, just having to take care of my part of the world, so I didn't feel cheated and like I said, the salary was amazing.

Now I sit here each night, waxing and waning when I need to, watching over you, counting how many breaths you take from when you close your eyes each night to when you open them in the morning, how many dreams you have and making sure that after each one, the light of the moon guides you safely back to the bed you left.

I don't own a car or even really live a life any more.

But I do have a lot of job satisfaction.

<4 comments>

Iain S. Thomas @IWroteThisForU - Jan 31
I've promised people I'll do things but I'm also still in bed
and it's this tension that will eventually destroy all of us.

To: Iain S. Thomas
From: Sandra J.
re: NEW BOOK!

Iain,

You still haven't sent anything. Noticed you had the time to write a whole story on your blog about someone riding a comet and lighting up the moon. Pretty. But also not making you or us any moneeeyyy.

Giving your writing away for free is fine but please also do the writing we're paying you to do. Advance should have already gone through.

We need to move on this.

Kind Regards, Sandra

Iain S. Thomas @IWroteThisForU - Feb 5
So much is done out of fear.

Iain S. Thomas @IWroteThisForU - Feb 5
"Here is a picture of my car because I'm afraid of what you think of my lifestyle."

Iain S. Thomas @IWroteThisForU - Feb 5
"Here is a comment about my relationship because what if you think I am not loved."

Iain S. Thomas @IWroteThisForU - Feb 5
"Here is a comment about my holiday because I worry that you think I don't travel."

To: Sandra J.
From: Iain S. Thomas
re: NEW BOOK!

Hi Sandra,

Yes, got the money, yes, paid the rent and the bills and everything else. Sorry I didn't send anything through sooner, just trying to find my way through all this. I think this might be a better attempt at it.

Writing doesn't pay much and as I've mentioned before I'm taking corporate jobs writing ad copy here and there to pay bills. I had to come up with a name for a soda the other day. It was meant to be sold to kids but the name couldn't say, "This is for kids." I told them I was a writer, not a wizard. Got fired.

I got married, as you know. Weddings aren't cheap. Thank you for the advance but even with that, I am dogged by money or at least the lack of it.

I'm thinking about doing a small book of poems about my wife. Maybe we can sell that? Everything's for sale, I don't care what. Did I ever tell you how hard my father worked so we'd be ok? That's what I think of artistic integrity. Please, sell something, because I want to take care of my family.

New draft of the happy book is also attached, as are the poems about my wife I mentioned. I really hope it's what you're looking for; I do know it was what I was looking for when I wrote it.

Anyway, this is what I found.

Keep well, Iain

How To Be Happy.

Don't seek out things that you hate and adopt them like children, devoting your life to hating something.

Unless it's cancer or racism or sexism or rape or North Korea's complete and utter brutalisation of its own people. It's ok to hate those things. In fact, you should hate those things.

Pour the hate down on those things from the highest rooftop.

But don't find an actor you don't like or a restaurant or a person and then spend all your time complaining. Just don't watch their movies or eat at the restaurant or hang out with them - you'd be happier if you were eating at a restaurant that actually made you happy, that cooked food that made you think of your mother and the way she used to cook for you when you were a child.

I think that's a good thing to say but I don't really know. My mother's best dish is just a grilled cheese sandwich but my God, it's the best grilled cheese sandwich I've ever tasted.

Head towards things you love, head away from things you hate.

You'd think natural human instinct would ensure that we do that but apparently not, some of us love the things we hate. We hang around, looking for new ways to hate, new ways to find some kind of purpose in the hate because the hate makes us feel like we're doing something. Like we're in motion even if we're just standing still, holding a big, heavy bucket of hate.

Maybe we are all doomed from the start.

No.

I didn't mean to say that. I meant, maybe we all have choices that we have to make from the start and then keep making them every day we want to keep being, us.

The same choices over and over again make you, you.

That's worth remembering, these are all choices we make. Nobody holds a gun to our head to force us to be us. We just are.

There's nothing wrong with seeing a shrink. A therapist. A psychologist. A counsellor. Whatever you want to call it. There's nothing wrong with paying someone good money to just shut up and listen to you go on about your life and then say, "You've been talking about your father for two hours straight, do you think you might have an issue with your father?" and then you go, "Well, I'd never really considered that, maybe you're right." Maybe it makes you feel better to be able to give a name to the stuff that makes you sad.

Maybe.

Maybe to give names to the things that make us happy and the things that make us sad, makes us human.

Just feel the things you need to feel, whatever their names are.

Whatever you do, don't ignore them. More importantly, don't beat yourself up for the way you feel, there's nothing worse than feeling bad for feeling bad, like you have no right to feel bad. You do, you have every right to feel bad and sometimes, you just need to feel bad for a little while before you can feel good again.

Just don't forget to feel good again. Like I said, sometimes we aren't very good at remembering to be happy.

I think being human would be boring if we were always one way or another, we wouldn't know what happiness felt like if we didn't know what sadness felt like and vice versa. Somewhere in the tension between these two points, is life.

Maybe every feeling has a reason for being.

I think sadness is there to make us avoid the things that are bad for us.

Sadness is a way for the person deep down inside you to take care of you, the person desperately trying to keep you alive despite everything. They reach out from the dark inside you and pinch your heart between their fingers so that you'll stop whatever you're doing and look around you, and wonder why your heart feels so very, very sore.

I'm sorry for all the self-awareness and the fact that a book about being happy isn't actually very happy, I really am, especially considering I said earlier on to watch out for irony, which is a killer. I'm honestly not trying to be ironic, I'm never even really sure what that word means beyond that Alanis Morissette song. Although the examples she uses seem to be more tragic than anything else.

Why won't someone just give her a knife? Why won't someone help the poor lady out instead of making fun of her for her choice of words?

I get really angry at people who are mean to other people. Isn't life hard enough without people making it worse for each other? I think the people who do, who set out to make others feel bad, feel bad and alone themselves, and they don't want to feel alone, so they make other people feel bad. So they'll just feel bad but also maybe, not so alone.

The people who are mean to you desperately want you to love them and be near them, is what I'm saying.

That's why we always gravitate to people that can do that, people like Nelson Mandela or Gandhi, who, even though horrible things happened to them, can still love because that's really, really hard, and you have to respect people who are doing that when you see it.

I'm sure they hurt too and sometimes, they even got really angry at taxi drivers who cut them off and yelled at them from their car when no one could hear them, I'm sure at one point in Gandhi's life, he wanted to yank someone out of their car on the freeway for cutting him off. But maybe he also knew that he was some kind of ideal for a lot of people, some kind of example of how we all could be. And that means that he and others like him always had to love when people were looking at them, and even when they weren't, just in case someone really was and they hadn't spotted them yet.

Maybe some people are loving and good all the time, but I think that's almost impossible. It's impossible for me. I don't know if you have the same problems as me.

I don't know you and I don't want to make assumptions about you (besides the fact that you might still feel ripped off if you bought this book, again, I'm really sorry if that happened).

I think that's enough for now. I'm going to walk away from this now and come back to it later, I'm just tired. If I delete everything, maybe that'd be better. I can just look at this as some kind of exercise or something.

Maybe.

I don't know.

I'm sorry.

Here are some things you can try at home.

• Think of all the different people you could be. Write their names down on pieces of paper. Tear them up. Be only you, forever.

• Pretend your entire life has been easy. Think about what kind of person you'd be if that were true. Think about, if you had to choose between the person you are and the person you'd be if your entire life had been easy, which one you'd prefer to be.

• Learn to play an instrument badly. Try and create some kind of noise with the instrument that doesn't make traditional musical sense. Make your own kind of music instead. Later, if you feel like it, watch some lessons on YouTube.

• Touch your hands.

• Keep a diary of every negative feeling you have. At the end of each day, try and work out which ones serve a purpose. Keep those, discard the rest.

Darling, I'm Drunk

I've read every book in this house
Listened to every song
I've played all these games before
And I don't have the guts to start
Building a model ship without you
   If there's something in this house
That'll make me happy
Without you
I haven't found it yet
   And every stranger at the mall
Looks at me and asks,
   "Who are you missing? Why are you here?"
   And I wish there was a way to eat alone, with other people, without
them seeing you.
   And when you drink whiskey out the bottle, the hill you're standing
on gets steeper.
   I wrote down a sentence
"A poem is just a song you don't sing,"
And I think I'll make that one a song
And I wish I could tell you that in person
   There's snow on the mountains
It's beautiful, crisp and sunny in Cape Town
   I hope it's better in New York.

Amanda, The Moon And Me

Amanda, I saw the man you're going to marry
Just hours before you
He was laying his head down
To sleep
(he said)
"Moon, tell Amanda I saw you and remind her that
when she sees you,
she must remember that our eyes saw the same light,
(no matter how far apart
we are,
the light,
is,
the,
same)."
Amanda, the man you're going to marry
feeds the dogs and the cat
and he doesn't mind
because he spends his time
thinking
of
you
(he said)
"Moon, tell Amanda that time passes differently, it goes
slower when we're far
and too fast when we're not,
things are always changing,
(but at least,
the moon,
stays,
the,
same)."

Amanda, the man you're going to marry
hates how quiet the house is
and the animals crowd around
when your voice
comes
over
the
speakers
　　(he said)
　　"Moon, tell Amanda, the man who's going to marry her
loves her,
he misses her
(and he knows
you feel,
the,
same)."

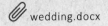

Wedding Poem

"You need to write something for the priest to say."
She knows I should write it. And it sounds so easy
Because I write so much. But what she's saying is
"Write the most beautiful thing you've ever written.
Try and capture a single moment of all I mean to you
With nothing but the noise your pen makes."
And she knows how much inside myself I am
And she pulls me out.
And how do I explain to everyone how many little things like that
There are.

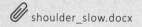

Shoulder, Shoulder, Slow, Slow

I had this dream that we somehow evolved without vocal chords

And the only way we could talk to each other was by touching our own or each other's skin

And entire books were written entirely in hugs and hand holding and letting go of each other

And we'd hold and touch and let go of each other in all these different ways to say all these different things

And when Neil Armstrong landed on the moon he just put his hand over his heart and held it there with his other hand and it said everything to everyone watching at home

And the news presenter did the same and so did everyone else

And there are museums you can go to, in my dream, where they have a set of mechanical hands and you put them against your heart and you can hear his exact words as he said them

And when people got married everyone just held each other's hands in a circle and cried and all the funerals in my dream looked exactly the same

And the people with the lightest fingers spoke so softly

And fishermen and workers had low gravelly voices

And I dreamed this dream for so long, I learned how to speak entirely in touch

And I write poetry on my wife's back every evening before she sleeps

And her skin and her nerve endings are a kind of paper that only remembers the ink written on it for a moment

And while it loses something in my terrible translation, my favourite work goes

"Shoulder, shoulder, slow, slow, neck, arm, back, curve, slow, slow, shoulder, shoulder, slow, slow, neck, arm, back, curve, slow, slow."

And it is so much more eloquent than anything I've ever said and so much more beautiful than anything I've ever written, with words.

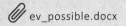

Everything Else Is Disposable

Most other people smile with all the sincerity of trend forecasters.
Most encourage others softly, like with a retweet of something they said five days ago.
Most hope their lives will be shared, like an exciting link to something that no one would believe.
I'm happier than them all though, because I kiss my wife like a running shoe commercial.

While You Sleep

    The big wooden heart
We keep in the hallway
Fell over and made the loudest noise
And I cried
    I was dreaming
I was driving down the highway
With the top down
And each bump in the road
Was a kick drum
And I was without you
And it felt like I was
Covered in flames
    I woke up
When the wooden heart fell
And had a shower
And the post-it notes
You left on the mirror
Fell
Like leaves in a river
    Wake up and come home
I want to tell you
It'll all be ok
    You're the only one I've told
Why I can't tell anyone
Anything
At
All

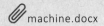

This Machine

I'm going to go back to college to study engineering.
I'm going to study medicine and find out
how those little pads they put on sick people work.
I'm going to stay up all night studying
until I know absolutely everything there is to know
about bodies and wires
and then I'm going to build a machine that lets me take
someone else's pain
and I will take everything you're feeling
away from you
I will take
every piece of broken glass in your heart
and put it into mine
because you have become a bigger part of me
than I am to myself
because being able to take your pain for you
is the only thing that'll make me feel better.
So I'm going back to college.

February 18, 2014

To: Iain S. Thomas
From: Sandra J.
re: NEW BOOK! - WHAT?!

Iain.

I beg you. Don't do this. Book is ridiculous, don't pretend you don't see that. Passed it around the office.

Girl went home crying.

Starting to worry you're actively trying to write a bad book.

Delete this, start again, keep the little ideas that work and try and expand on them.

Also, saw your short 'story' in Hero Magazine. More writing that isn't for us?

Kind Regards, Sandra

TALKING TO STRANGERS IS HOW YOU MAKE FRIENDS

BY IAIN S. THOMAS

There's nothing to do and it drives you inside, into the dark with the curtains drawn on bright days, into secret alliances and friendships. It breeds a kind of creativity born of desperation. So you learn how computers work or you blow things up or you take drugs but you find something to obsess over because you need something to do.

There's something quite mad that comes out of here and if necessity is the mother of invention, small town streets are filled with her lonely sons and daughters.

Small towns are a contradiction. They detest difference but below the surface, this lack of acceptance creates it. So in the time of this story, we're all different and weird and none of us are really welcome here.

It's 1994 and my brother, David, has a habit of chewing his thumb while he thinks and he leaves his body behind completely when he's absorbed in something, which is usually a book or a screen.

A new computer arrives one day with a demo of a 3D rotating clown head and we sit in front of the monitor watching it turn. I don't think we'd be shocked if somebody came back from the future and said, "This is what a PS4 looks like," because we know, we can see the future in that clown's head.

This is Port Elizabeth, South Africa. Detroit by the sea. Everyone's dad works for a car factory. General Motors changes their name to Delta, to get around the Apartheid sanctions, so my dad works for General Motors and then Delta without ever leaving the building. The streets always feel deserted and there are coal dumps next to the beach.

Right now, there are two men from Interpol outside our front door and in a few seconds, they'll knock and everything will change. See, David worked out how to make free phone calls using a program called Blue Box and made a deal with a guy running a phone sex operation in Bulgaria that was going to make both of them rich, but they're about to get caught. He's 16. I am walking through the house in my boxer shorts because I'm 14 years old and I've just woken up, because I've spent the entire night talking to strangers online. Talking to someone else over a phone line is a novelty, it's weird, it's strange and you can do it all night.

I will be depressed in 16 years time when the internet is just a ubiquitous thing, nothing more magical than a chair or a bar of soap. Too much William Gibson and Cyberpunk 2020.

They knock on the door, I answer and I don't see their guns and they ask me, "We've got a search warrant for your premises, do you have any computer software or hardware?" Everyone will laugh, years from now, because I say, "Mom, it's for you." My mother doesn't know anything about computers. She wears a straw hat in the kitchen to protect herself from the cancer-causing UV rays from the halogen tubes in the light.

They go past her to the back of the house where the computer is and one of my brother's friends eats a piece of paper with phone numbers written on it.

They arrest my brother and it's over. The computer will come back in a few months with a case number scrawled down the side in black marker.

But David never stops loving machines. In 18 years' time, he will work in the technological heart of a bank and make more money than God. I will never stop chasing the spiritual, divine experience of talking to strangers and I become a writer and I don't make more money than God but I talk to thousands of people every day that I don't know and it fills me with electricity and makes me feel human. Like there's a small town for people like me.

In 2015, there's a guy wishing he could send a message back saying, "Don't be afraid of being weird. Everyone else is just normal. You get out of here one day."

I just don't know that right now.

Iain S. Thomas is a poet, author and co-creator of the world-renowned blog and bestselling book, I Wrote This For You

Iain S. Thomas @IWroteThisForU - Feb 19
The problem with the chemicals in my head is they lead to
feelings in the rest of me.

Here at last, we shall be free.

Some Things Which Once Made Me Happy

In Uncategorized on February 20, 2014 at 11:56pm

New vinyl smell. Rain on a windscreen (windscreen wipers). Dog-eared books. Spelling a word right the first time you write it. Someone else's hair in your face. 12:00am. 11:11pm. Acoustic guitars. No top. Bubble wrap. Hot weather at 1:00am. The muscles in your shoulders. Empty roads on the way home. Sitting upside down, staring out the windshield in the passenger seat. A comment on your wall. Inside jokes. Sugar. Candles and power failures. Knowing where you'll be a week from now. The expected, unexpected. Dichotomy. Serendipity. Words ending on an "e" sound. The whole day is in bed.

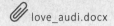

Love, Audi

I have trouble saying my own name and yet no trouble saying yours.
I would call things and people by different names, we all would, if we could.
We all do when we're inside ourselves.
I never really learnt how to say it and
whenever I give my name to the pizza place there's always a question mark at the end of it.
I am expecting them to say, "What?"
But I still brush my teeth every morning because I want to be a better person.
(We all measure happiness in displacement, by what gaps the things that leave us, leave).
(Try to try more times than you fail).
There're so many stupid conferences you can go to
to learn how to sell stupid things to stupid people.
Everyone's profile picture is just them with a shit-eating-grin.
I don't know what else it should be.
Maybe a picture of themselves with the thing that hurt them.
So often the thing that hurts you is the thing that makes you human.
As you get older you miss people you didn't think you would.
That one popular kid from high school has had a child
(we were all kids once)
and you think, "Good for him."
The guy who made my iPhone probably killed himself;
I wonder if his ghost listens to my calls.
If he sends Morse code messages over
the static on the line
if the call drops
he probably just doesn't like what I'm saying.
None of us are so brave any more.
Not because misery loves company
but because misery is so comfortable.
They're building cars that drive themselves;
one day a car will shoot itself in the bonnet;
it'll send a text to your smartwatch that says
"I'm so sorry, goodbye.
Love, Audi."

To: Sandra J.
From: Iain S. Thomas
re: NEW BOOK! - Changed to Sacred Grammar

Sandra,

I'm not in a good place. I'm trying to find my way through this thing but it's not happening. I'm lost and the compass is spinning. I feel like something is chasing me through the darkness. It might be the darkness itself. Maybe it's something that's been following me my whole life.

Did I ever tell you about the time I played Follow The Leader when I was a child? I dove through a plate-glass window to stop the other kids from following me. That's how I won. I got 10 stitches across my head. I'm petrified some days that I'm not real. Isn't that every artist's fear? That they're not authentic and original? What if I'm just following something?

I keep having this dream where a German car shoots itself in the bonnet and then my smartwatch beeps. It's hard for me to write about being happy right now.

I got up in the middle of the night and started writing something else. It's called "Sacred Grammar" - the basic idea is I take unicode symbols, you know those strange symbols you can make on the computer like ◊? And I give them meaning. I just want something to mean something and maybe this is a way to give that to a thing. I'm just trying to find shapes and fill them with something true.

I'd like to do this instead of the how to be happy book. Sorry, I know.

Also, no comment on the poems about my wife? Please respond soonest.

Keep well, Iain

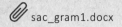
SACRED GRAMMAR #1: Î

"Î"

Used to mark a sentence that neither starts nor ends, or to indicate possession of the sun, moon and stars.

For example:

"I will wait for you here Î"

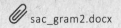

SACRED GRAMMAR #2: Ó

"ó"

Indicates shock and surprise at how important someone or something has become to your life at the point at which they or it are no longer there.

For example:

"Ó ... when are you coming back?"

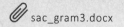

SACRED GRAMMAR #3: *

"*"

Refers to the star a person becomes when they live a life and become the centre point of a collection of people and experiences that make them who they are.

It can be described as simply who and what they pull together to become something new.

For example:

"All the photos on your hard drive, anyone you've ever touched, with a hand or a word, your feelings, the sky and the ocean, you are the * that binds them all together."

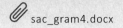
SACRED GRAMMAR #4: Σ

"Σ"

Used to indicate a constant rising of the spirit, a desire to leave the body and float above it for a moment, to stand in awe at the majesty of the universe.

For example:

"He walked outside after everyone else had gone to sleep and looked up. Despite what had happened, beneath the billions of stars, in the silence of the night, he felt a constant Σ"

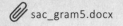

SACRED GRAMMAR #5: ◊

"◊"

The act of taking what you feel and making it nothing. Like light made small.

For example:

"You whisper "shhh" to yourself, you hold yourself inside yourself, you ◊."

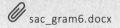
SACRED GRAMMAR #6: ≅

"≅"

When the more people you meet, the more you enjoy time on your own. To crave your own space.

For example:

"I would go out tonight but ≅ I can't."

To: Iain S. Thomas
From: Sandra J.
re: NEW BOOK! - Changed to Sacred Grammar

Iain.

No, we can't make a new book about characters that no one uses.
I don't always understand your stuff but this is too far - even for you.

You cannot back out of the Happy Book. This was your idea, we've
paid you, you owe us a book. This will become a legal matter if you
don't supply us with that book. Didn't want things to get to this kind
of a place but that needs to be said.

Wish things were heading on a more even keel for you but this is the
way of the world. Reworking title to "The Real Secret Of Happiness,
Be Happy Today!"

I think you'll agree it's better. Can talk about all these other ideas
another time.

Attached is the cover. Will inspire you - maybe?

Kind Regards, Sandra

SOON TO BE A MAJOR MOTION PICTURE

THE PERFECT GIFT FOR THE SAD PERSON IN YOUR LIFE!

GET RID OF YOUR DEPRESSION INSTANTLY WITH THESE HANDY TIPS!

If you're not happy and you know it, buy this book!

Not happy? What the hell is wrong with you?!

How to Be HAPPY!!

THE REAL SECRET OF HAPPINESS, BE HAPPY TODAY!
A MAP TO YOUR OWN PERSONAL HAPPY PLACE!
EXERCISE YOUR HAPPY MUSCLES!

Iain S. Thomas

Here at last, we shall be free.

WHO?   FOLLOW ME - I'M GOING TO GET CANDY   BUY SOME BOOKS   ARCHIVES   RSS FEED

A Water Cooler Somewhere In Hell

In Uncategorized on March 3, 2014 at 3:57am

"If you make me sick, please don't make me better."

Is a bumper sticker, you would do well in the bumper sticker industry

You could become head of bumper sticker technology

And one day, while you're all laughing at the water cooler

At your jobs at the bumper sticker factory

You'll turn to the guy next to you, drinking coffee

In your striped and collared shirts

Laughing, slapping each other's backs and one of

You, one of you will say

"You know, I bet many people scream with their last breath

'I'll tell the truth tomorrow.'"

And all of you will entirely deserve the awkward silence that follows.

Iain S. Thomas @IWroteThisForU - Mar 5
Each person on Earth should be assigned another person,
and we should all apologise to each other, once a day, for
all the stupid shit.

To: Sandra J.
From: Iain S. Thomas
re: NEW BOOK! - Cover Issues

Sandra.

I've spent the money you've sent and so I guess I don't really have a choice. I'll work on the book but I'd rather not. If I'm going to do it, it's going to be my book. It's attached.

I feel like the cover is completely wrong. I've got another one I want to use. It's an illustration from an old medical textbook from the American Civil War. It's a kind of torch you can make with rope, in an emergency, if you need to perform surgery in the dark in the middle of a war. I feel like it's a good indication of what I'm trying to do. I just want people to have some light somewhere that they can use. Even on a battlefield. Even if their hands are covered in blood.

I also wrote a short story about how strange it is that we can't all just be nice to each other. It's 2014 and we're still fighting over all the same stupid shit we've been fighting over for the last few thousand years. Doesn't that depress you? We're never going to leave Earth. Maybe that's what happened to every planet that could support life. Cells divided and divided and divided until they were conscious and then they looked at each other and forgot that they came from the same place, that we all have the same mother and father. And then we all kill each other until there's nothing left to kill.

Anyway, this story isn't aimed at you, I'm just talking generally.

Will keep trying,

- Iain

P.S. Also made some comics on my iPad which are attached. As I mentioned, I do need some money, so maybe you can sell them to a newspaper or something? They'd work right next to Garfield.

HOW TO BE HAPPY...

Again.

Never try and fix something with a gun.

You can't fix anything with a gun unless something doesn't have enough holes in it. Unless it's a bucket shower or a bag over your head that's stopping you from breathing, very few things need more holes in them in order to be fixed.

Never scream "I hate everything and I just wish the pain would stop, I want it to end, I want everything to end!" because that sounds like you might kill yourself and then people have every right to put you in a fancy white jacket and leave you in a padded room.

Again, I don't know you but most people won't be happy alone in a padded room, unless you like jumping castles, in which case, maybe you want to go into that room and just bounce around for a while, knowing that nothing you do will hurt you.

Remember that memory is 'state-specific.' Don't worry, I didn't know what the hell that meant either when I first heard it but someone explained it to me once.

When you're sad, you only remember sad things and when you're happy, you only remember happy things.

That's why when you're really sad, it feels like your whole life has just been one big sad thing that doesn't ever let up with the sadness and your brain goes,

"Remember when your dad wasn't there, that was sad, and that time those kids made fun of you for peeing in your pants, that was sad too, and by the way, nothing happy has ever happened in between any of these events."

Your brain can be an asshole like that.

Which is scary because your brain just listens to whatever you tell it, so if you keep telling it, "You're a moron who can't do anything right," your brain will say, "Ok cool, I'm a moron who can't get anything right, I'll remember that the next time I'm trying to not be a moron and trying to get something right."

So say nice things to your brain. Tell your brain you love it. Tell your brain you've always admired it from afar. Tell your brain that if you could take it on a date, you would. You would buy it nice things and read it poetry next to a rainy window. Mean it when you say it.

Say nice things to your heart.

Sometimes I like to picture myself as a kid and then I imagine that I give myself a hug but then I start crying and I have to say sorry to the kid in my head, even though it's just me imagining him, because kids get scared when grown-ups, the people who are supposed to know what the hell is going on, cry.

Grown-ups shouldn't cry in front of kids.

They should just always be ok, because the kids will think, "One day I'm going to be a grown-up and I want everything to be ok when I am and if everything is still messed up when I get older, then what's the point?"

So don't cry in front of a kid, even if the kid is actually just imaginary and in your head. They don't deserve that. Kids deserve better. The world is so hard, kids should spend as much time as possible not knowing just how hard it can really be, otherwise they'll become hard little grown-ups before they've had a chance to be happy little kids.

I'm glad there are kids in the world. They give us a reason to be strong and they give us something to protect and everyone needs something to be strong for and something to protect, even if it's just their own heart, or the kid in their head.

Ok.

Do really difficult things in the morning.

If you do really difficult things in the morning then when they're ☐ done you can feel really good about yourself, because they're done, and the rest of the day doesn't seem so bad. If you get up early enough, it's like you're not even really doing it because you're tired and not really awake yet, so it's not like you're actually doing it and you'll probably forget how hard it was, because you're a different person when you wake up completely to the person you are when you're tired and don't really know what's going on.

Make art.

Take the thing that hurts you inside and bring it outside yourself, sing it out, write it out, paint it out, dance it out, it doesn't matter if it's technically good or not, it becomes 'good' art simply because it helped you move through whatever you were going through.

But don't try to manufacture pain just to be able to sell it.

Don't try to force yourself into a dark place because you think there's really nice art inside it. Dark places are dark to warn us away from them. If the world pushes you somewhere dark, fine, go there and use the art to get yourself out again, just don't go in there intentionally looking for a tragedy for your canvas.

When you're painting a sunset, red paint is fine, it doesn't need to be blood.

Listen, I'm feeling a little better today so hopefully all this stuff is helpful on some level and maybe you don't feel as ripped off as you did in that other chapter, which if all goes to plan, won't be published when this book is. (Delete this line.)

Understand that a real relationship, real love, is accepting that you're going to watch someone you really care about waste away.

To drown in time and themselves.

You and the person you love play chicken with the length of your lives, to see who'll die first. Which of you will have the grim task of putting the other into the ground? Which of you will say goodbye, alone?

That's why it's not fair to smoke. It's not fair. That's cheating.

Don't do drugs. Unless it's aspirin for a headache or your therapist puts you on antidepressants, then it's ok. Otherwise, drugs will make you think you're ok when you're really not and worse, they can make you feel ok even though you're in a bad situation and the reason you feel bad when you're in a bad situation is that person in your head or in your heart or wherever they find themselves right now, the one trying to keep you alive, wants you to stop hurting yourself, so they reach up, out of the dark, one more time, and they pinch your heart, or give you a stomach ache, or play drums until four in the morning with the thoughts that keep beating away in your head.

Drugs also make the people around you feel horrible because when you take drugs, it says to them "Where I am now, just isn't good enough. You're not good enough people to make me happy, I have to take a chainsaw to my brain chemistry and alter it enough so that I no longer know who or what I am, because right now, I don't like who or what I am."

That's a horrible thing to hear. Even if you don't say it out loud, your behaviour says it for you.

I really hope you aren't on drugs right now because then I've probably really, really, really ruined your day and if you thought this was a book you could take drugs and read, then you were mistaken and I am truly sorry.

Risk doing the things that'll make you happy.

It's always a risk worth taking and if you don't and someone asks you one day why you didn't, then you'll just burst into tears and keep saying, "I don't know, I don't know."

Crying in front of the people you love hurts but maybe if you're lucky, those people love you too, and they're ok with you crying and they'll squeeze your hand really tightly and pull you close and whisper again and again in your ear, "It's ok. It's ok."

Even if it isn't. Because that's what the people who love you do.

To have someone whisper, "It's ok. It's ok," in your ear is a very human kind of happiness.

If you're not happy when you have nothing, nothing is going to change that.

You can have a big yacht and an apartment made of glass and chrome, or maybe even an apartment on a yacht made of glass and chrome, but that's not going to make you happy if you weren't happy before you got it.

Unless of course you were just looking for a place to sleep, a place to feel ok for a while. But then if you're in that situation, it wouldn't really matter what the apartment was made out of or whether it was on a yacht or in the sky or wherever.

My point is, things (like stuff) don't make you happy, no matter how much of them you have.

You will never feel a sense of satisfaction as you're walking around your estate with a journalist, saying, "This is my thing collection. These are some of the finest things money can buy and I keep them all here and pay a man to come around on Mondays and polish all the things, isn't that impressive?"

Even if the journalist nods and scribbles some notes about your thing collection, if you weren't happy before you got the things, you won't be happy now either. Even if the journalist writes for the most important magazine in the world.

I know I'm about to repeat myself but some of this is important, more important than a glass of water or exercise, and it's important to me that you understand.

Trying to be successful and trying to accomplish something are both great things to do and you should do those things if you think they'll fill up a part of you that needs filling up, but don't do things just for money. Unless, like I said, you think money is the thing that'll make you happy. I don't think it will, but you and me, maybe we're different.

Which brings me to this: While we all share fundamental, common experiences, everyone is not the same.

Just because you feel things a certain way doesn't mean everyone feels them the same way too. Sometimes the problem isn't that we should treat others as we'd want to be treated, the problem is that we do, and we don't realise that actually, we should treat others how they want to be treated.

While we can each be in love, we can express our love in completely different ways. We can experience happiness doing totally different things. There is no better or worse. There's only us and the things we do to reach beyond ourselves for something better.

Understanding this is called empathy. For example, there's a guy who was reading this earlier and he's given up, he's feeling completely and utterly ripped off, and he's slammed down this book and gone for a smoke or a drive or something to calm down - he's given up but you're still here because you and him, you are different.

Unless you are that guy and you didn't go for a smoke and you are actually still here, in which case, I'm sorry for talking about you behind your back.

Sorry.

You're probably already paranoid about the world being out to get you and here comes this stupid book talking about you while it thinks you're away doing something else. Just don't take it as a sign or an indicator that the delusion you hold of the world being out to get you is true.

Do you have any idea how many people there are in the world and how much coordination it would take to focus all our energy on one guy without him knowing?

We can't even agree on what to do about global warming! What makes you think we could hatch a plot against just you? How special would you have to be for the whole world to plot against you? And while it'll have your back, you're not special to the world. You're special to you. And that's ok.

Don't watch old movies with actors in them that you've always loved and felt really close to and then google them and find pictures of how they look today, because they always look older, and then you'll start to wonder when they'll die.

They don't even know you.

They were like an uncle or an aunt you didn't have, and they made you laugh and cry so many times and they don't even know you and now time has taken so much away from them and they might die soon and you'll never get to tell them how much they meant to you.

For God's sake, don't do that.

They'd probably want you to be happy for the good times you shared in front of the TV. If they knew you. Which they don't.

Don't try and exchange niceness for love.

They're two completely different things. You should be nice because you want to be nice, not because you expect to be loved in return. Yelling at someone, "But I was nice to you! You owe me love now!" is a surefire way to make people think, "That guy's not very nice at all, ironically."

For the record, I do know that dramatic irony is what happens when you're watching a show and the audience knows something that the characters the actors are playing don't.

Like when you see two people hurting each other but you can see they both love each other, and you just wish they would stop hurting each other.

Although I don't know if that's the same thing. Maybe.

Don't think about all your exes when you're lonely, you're not remembering the fights or how every gift they bought you was something they really liked but you didn't.

You're not thinking about sleeping on opposite sides of the bed and how cold everything was.

You're just remembering coffee and movies and things. You're just remembering some of the things. Not all of the things. State-specific memory is pretty much that.

To have state-specific memory is human or something and to be human is to remember things that hopefully once made us happy.

Is any of this even making sense any more?

Here are some things you can try at home.

• What would your perfect day look like? Not if you had all the money in the world, or if you could do anything and you knew you wouldn't fail - look at the life you lead right now and work out, with the 24 hours you have, what would be the best, most satisfying use of your time. Write it down.

• Look at the exercise you've done above. Consider why you haven't left any time at all for rest and reflection. For doing nothing. For just being a human. For sitting and thinking. Sit and think about that.

• If your body was inhabited by someone you really respected and admired, how would you treat them? Why don't you treat yourself like that? If the person you loved and admired the most was coming over to visit, what would your home look like? Look around you, and ask important questions.

Here is a drawing. I hope it makes you happy.

FOLLOW

your

DREAMS

BUT WEAR YOUR PANTS IN ALL OF THEM

iain
thomas

I ~~have~~ cut off larger parts of me.

I have this dream where I'm in a dancing competition with everyone who has ever upset me.

I win and then I Forgive them.

iain
thomas

Lets be
beautiful and
new together

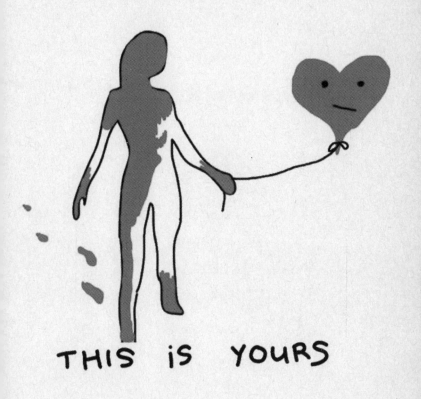

THIS IS YOURS

(Don't actually do this. This is an art thing.)

No one knows but...

sometimes I drive into rush hour traffic even when I don't have to.

Just so I'll have people around me.

iain thomas

I don't understand
why we wait for
a funeral to
say what we
should say
sooner.

Maybe
we
Become
birds
when
we
Die.

jon
thomas

you can't make me beg for

my dignity.

iain
thomas

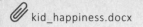

The Kid That Caused Unhappiness

Some homeless guy first found the kid. Nearly flipped his lid. Ran up to me and said, "Listen to the crazy shit this kid is spewing," which coming from a homeless guy, reeking of cigarettes and stale booze, is a pretty bold statement. So I humoured him and said ok, then turned to the kid. What he said next nearly destroyed the world.

"What if we were all just nice to each other?"

It may seem like a pretty common idea now but back then, you got to remember, we were killing each other 'n warring 'n raping the earth, not all peaceful like it is now. So I ask him to repeat himself and he says, "I said, what if we were all just nice to each other?"

So I phone the Chief of Police and get him out here to listen to this kid's crazy political theory, some kind of socialisitimarxisidemocracticthingamaboo that just doesn't seem to make sense even though it does.

Chief comes down with a couple of SWAT teams to see what's going on. By now, there's a bit of a crowd around the kid, and he's a dirty little bastard in some torn jeans and what used to be a white t-shirt with some fucked up sneakers and a runny nose and the crowd's doing that, raarraarrarararr, low-mosquito noise. The chief yells, "What the hell's going on here?"

"This kid's lost his mind, Chief," says one of the cops who got there first.

"You called me out here for a kid? Throw him in the back of a van and get him to a home or something, I haven't got time for shit like this."

"No, Chief, listen to what the kid's got to say."

"This better be fucking amazing, son, or you're going to be working security at a fucking lemonade stand once I'm done with you."

"It is, Chief, listen to him."

Chief turns to the kid and says, "Ok, kid, let's have it. What you got to say?"

"I said," and he clears his throat, "what if we were all just nice to each other?"

At that moment a bead of sweat was born on the Chief's forehead and I swear I saw it happen. I could see the cogs in his head working and the little puffs of steam coming out his ears.

Ten minutes later, there's a black helicopter touching down in the middle of the street and guys in black suits and black sunglasses hop out and grab the kid, all civilised because obviously we're all watching to see what's going to happen, which is nothing because once he's in the helicopter, they take off again. That's the last we ever saw of that kid.

I heard that they took him to see the president. Then they took him to this tiny little cement room down in the bottom of the building, and shot him in the back of the head.

It was a while before we managed to get the word out about what the kid said, but we did and the world changed.

You'd best be grateful for what that kid did.

March 31, 2014

To: Iain S. Thomas
From: Sandra J.
re: NEW BOOK! - Cover Wrong!

Iain.

Saw you posted the book cover to Facebook. Not the cover we sent you? Makes it look like you've written a book about candles.

Not looking at the other attachments. Book is completely wrong. Spoke to someone about you. They said maybe you have some kind of penniless poet fantasy. That the idea of being a starving artist appeals to you.

If you send me anything but the book we're asking for, the one we've paid you to write, I will help make this fantasy real.

Not happy. That's irony.

Kind Regards, Sandra

Iain S. Thomas @IWroteThisForU · Apr 4
If you stand out in the desert in the middle of the night and look at the stars, you can see the origin of every story ever written.

Iain S. Thomas @IWroteThisForU · Apr 4
I stargaze because it makes me, and my problems, feel so insignificant and small. I am a speck in a beam of light. Nothing matters.

May 1, 2014

To: Sandra J.
From: Iain S. Thomas
re: NEW BOOK! - Further Attachments

Sandra,

I'm trying to give you what you need, what people need, not what you're asking for. What you're asking for kills people. The inane, pseudo-bullshit of the world is what kills us.

Please see attached.

Keep well, Iain

How To Be Happy.

Again, again.

Maybe I should sort these out into headings and put tests and a synopsis at the end of each chapter, then I could sell it to those people who call everyone who reads their books dummies.

If you're not happy, I'm sorry, I don't think I can help you. I honestly thought this would be easier than it is and to be honest, I'm starting to think all I've really got is a huge bunch of things not to do, rather than a bunch of things you can do, which is going to be depressing for you, especially if you've read all this and realise you've had some of these experiences and nothing can be done and now you're just thinking, "Well, that ship has sailed."

Then you'll sigh and carry on reading but usually when people sigh, they're not happy. Although maybe they're just taking a deep breath. If someone isn't sad and they sigh and they're really just taking a deep breath and you ask them, "Why are you sad?" you'll make them sad, even if they weren't before, because now they're worried about what you think of them. I guess that's why sighing is the perfect passive/aggressive response to a situation because then if someone asks you, "Why are you so sad?"

You can easily say, "I'm not, I was just taking a deep breath, but thanks for killing my buzz, jerk."

Then the person asking you will feel bad, even though all they did was care about you.

Don't do that.

Just try and be good to one another.

Here are some things you can try at home.

• Imagine you're really happy. Write a letter to yourself to read when you're sad.

• Go through your cupboard. Give away anything that you don't wear any more.

• Try to greet every person on the street, especially people you wouldn't normally greet.

Here at last, we shall be free.

Suicide Is A Sin

In Uncategorized on June 1, 2014 at 10:02pm

She walks up to the counter
in her fucked-up skirt
and her fucked-up leggings
and her fucked-up Doc Martens
and points at each of the packs of cigarettes
"How much tar in that one?"
"And this one?"
"Does that one have filters?"
"I'm not a used-car salesman, pick a pack of cigarettes
and get out."
"I'm still not sure," she says, she's got her finger on her
cupid's bow.
She leans over and says, "Just tell me which one will
kill me the fastest."
The shopkeeper shakes his head and throws her a pack
of Texan Plain.
Years later she marvels at how she doesn't get change
for the note she slides
across the counter.
Years later she marvels at how she needs two notes
instead of one
to buy the same pack of Texan Plain.
Years later she's upset and confused and alone and she
hates herself but the person she hates the most
is the shopkeeper
and all his stupid, fucked-up broken promises.

<2 comments>

To: Sandra J.
From: Iain S. Thomas
re: NEW BOOK! - Please respond

Sandra,

I haven't heard anything back, I'm taking that as an indication that you've seen what I'm trying to do and everything's going ahead fine.

It's my birthday. As a present to you, I've written some stories about animals. I don't know why animals but it felt right, to give them a voice, to use them to try say some of the stuff I can't.

I'm in an awkward situation: I need more money. Could you please try and sell some of these animal stories to something that publishes stuff about animals, like maybe National Geographic?

Keep well, Iain

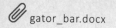

Gator In A Bar

You call it killing but it's just fighting till one of us dies. So I fight and I kill. And I'm a gator so you call it hunting because I eat what I kill. Would you feel better about yourselves if you ate what you killed or killed what you ate?

But humans are family, so one of your brothers kills your food for you. Or invents something that kills it and then gives it to another brother who gives it to another and another until you eat it. So you don't think "you" hunt.

I don't hunt any more. Not since you took me from the swamp. Put me here in this bar. In the pit. In the middle. You wrestle me, thinking you're tough. That wrestling a wild animal when you're drunk enough, out with your buddies or your bitch, makes you a man. From the sounds of things, that's something to be proud of. Doesn't count when you've ripped all my teeth out.

I'm an animal so I don't know if I'm capable of hate but if I am, then I hate you. You have become more than food to me. And I've noticed in your behaviour, the way you slouch against the bar, eyes like a cow's, that you are lazy. I smiled even though you wouldn't have noticed it, even if you'd looked. I smiled because I felt what could've been some miracle new tooth growing. Or maybe it's just bone rubbed free and clear from my featureless gums.

But it's there. My tongue knows it's there.

Now, while you clown around, putting your neck in my mouth, I'm getting ready to draw that sharpness, that last tiny spark of me still alive, across your throat. Then they'll shoot me. Then as you die, I will die. Shots ringing out will be the last thing I hear, your blood will be the last thing I taste and then I will be back in the swamp.

Beneath the water.

Happy.

Forever.

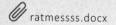

Rat In A Mess

So there I am right, running through this freaking maze because hey, it's what we always do and the time right now and at this point is; always. Whiskers a-twitter, I make it past the square bit through the more squiggly bit and into this long straight bit I hadn't been through, swing a sharp left and there it is.

Cheese.

Fucking cheese. I mean, don't get me wrong, I'm a rat, I love cheese, it makes me happy. I love cheese on Monday through Sunday and I love cheese on the in-between days, I love cheese on its own and I love cheese wrapped in cheese then deep fried in cheese and spread on cheese. Cheese is ok in my book.

But seriously, this is it? I've been running through the same fucking maze for months and now that I've done it, there's … cheese?

I'm thinking all this while I'm nibbling and it just gets to me, like, really gets to me. I'm sure 99% of all the other rats out there would be like, "Oh FUCK yeah, cheese," but maybe I'm just not 99% of all the other rats. So I say fuck the cheese. Fuck it. I'm not letting another fucking rat work and struggle and spend all that fucking time in that maze just so they can get a big piece of cheese.

I run back the way I came, I leave the cheese, because I know there's more suckers behind me and I figure they deserve a break, they should at least know, it's just a block of cheese.

The first rat I run into is one of those fresh-faced fuckers you always see in the sawdust, they think they're special, that they're chosen, instead of plucked.

I say, "Hey son, just so you know, if you keep going, if you ever make it all the way to the other end, it's just a block of cheese."

And he says, "You're trying to trick me, aren't you? You don't want to share the prize. You want to keep it to yourself. Well, tough luck, soldier, I'm smarter than you."

He bites my fucking leg, we tumble and we both end up the worse for wear, goes to show what trying to do someone a favour gets you. He skulks off, bleeding and squeaking, in the direction of his glorious fucking block of cheese and I do the same in the opposite direction.

Bleeding and more than a little fucked up, I get round this corner and there's this other rat, old guy, nervous, like the Woody Allen of rats and I tell him, "Listen, mister, I know you've been doing this your whole life and all, but if you ever do make it all the way through here, it's just a block of cheese."

He's freaked out. Like really freaked, I can tell because he shits himself right there and then. If I met me covered in blood and rambling about a block of cheese, I'd probably shit myself too.

"Thank you for your advice, sir, don't think for a single second I don't appreciate it but I'm afraid I don't really know anything else but this maze so if it's all the same to you, I'm going to carry on. Please don't hurt me."

So he scuttles past me, wet and reeking of fear. Fuck him.

I've lost a lot of blood at this point so I just drag my sorry rat ass forward, back the way I came, back past through the squiggly bit and the square bit and I realize I've never seen the maze from this angle before and everything's new and as I'm dragging and bleeding, I see a tail around a corner. I follow it, I figure I've got just enough blood left to tell one more rat and if I'm lucky, maybe they can tell the others.

So third rat, as we'll call her, is just wandering around sniffing the walls and there's some light coming in over the side and I think she can't be very smart because she's way, way, way off from the square bit and the squiggly bit that takes you to the long straight bit where the block of cheese is and maybe I shouldn't even bother telling her because she was never going to find it anyway but maybe one day she'll get lucky so what the hell.

"Hey, lady!" and she looks at me and runs over with these big red eyes and starts licking my wounds which I haven't really had time to do yet so it feels good and I figure maybe this rat isn't too bad.

"Thank you," I say, "but listen, I might not be here for much longer, I've lost a lot of blood and I really need to tell you something. At the end of the maze, if you make it all the way through, it's … it's just a block of cheese."

"But what else could it be?" she says. And I sigh because I've failed again for the last time and this is it, rats will be running through this goddamn fucking maze forever and what's worse, this rat is ok with the fact that it's a block of cheese.

"So you're going to carry on after the cheese?" I ask her.

"I was never after the cheese. I stay here. I've just always liked this part of the maze."

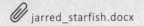

Starfish In A Jar

Once, when the sun was shining brightly upon the earth, a young girl went to the beach with her family. She played amongst the waves that ran their fingers along the sand, again and again. Soon, she went exploring and found a rock pool. In that rock pool, she found a starfish.

The starfish was not afraid when the young girl took it out of the water because it could sense the overwhelming love and wonder in her.

The young girl, wanting to take a part of the ocean home with her, put the starfish into a jar with some sand and some water.

At home that night, the starfish sat alone in the jar. A fly flew overhead and said, "You will die, beautiful starfish. A jar is not the ocean. Soon you will leave this place and go to the ocean that sits above the clouds. Soon your five legs will be still. Soon you will be no more."

"You are correct, fly. I will die. I have lived a good life though, and I am happy that at the end of it, I could satisfy the curiosity of a child and make her happy. I do, however, have one regret," replied the starfish.

"What is your regret, starfish? For though you and I are both very different, I am a good fly and do my best not to bother the animals around me, even the humans. I wish to help you," said the fly, buzzing over the jar.

The starfish laughed (as only a starfish can).

"You cannot help me, well-meaning fly. My regret is that I cannot dance one more time. Because to live in the ocean is to dance, constantly, to sway back and forth with the waves and the currents. To dance is to live, to be happy. But the only other animal a starfish can dance with is another starfish, and I am alone in this jar, where I will die."

The fly stopped buzzing, thoughtfully, and settled on the lip of the jar.

"I will do what I can, beautiful starfish," he said. And he flew away.

There was a corner in the house where no one ever looked. And though the fly knew that all his sisters and his brothers had always told him to stay away from that corner, he knew it was only in that corner that he could find help.

"Hello, spider," said the fly.

"Hello, fly. Have you come here to die?" asked the spider.

"It is not my time to die. It is another's. And they require your help to die," replied the fly.

"Why should I help another?" and the spider laughed, "I have all I need here in my web, I owe no one and nothing any favours."

"Yes," said the fly, "but you are lonely in your web. You have everything you need here, except company."

"I eat my company," said the spider.

"Yes you do. That is why you are lonely and unhappy," said the fly.

"Fine. I am, indeed, lonely and unhappy. But how will helping another keep me from being lonely or make me happy?" asked the spider.

"Because helping others is to help yourself. There is a dying starfish that wants one last dance before it passes on. You are the only animal here that can dance with it. I know you have never danced or met a starfish before. This will ease your loneliness, if only for a while," replied the fly.

The spider scowled as it was not used to having conversations with food.

"Enough of your lies. Either join me in my web or leave. I am weary now and wish to be alone," said the spider, skittering back to the centre of the web.

Sad, the fly flew away and left the spider to its loneliness.

Alone in its web, the spider thought and thought and thought about something it had never thought of before: being alone.

Slowly and cautiously, it left the web.

If you were lucky enough to be in the house that night, you would've seen a spider crawl across the ceiling and slowly, delicately lower itself into a jar with a starfish in it.

If you were lucky enough to be in the house that night, you would've seen how a starfish and a spider can dance (the three extra legs on the spider's part allow for some truly spectacular moves).

If you were lucky enough to be in the house that night, you would've seen them dance until there was no more night to dance in.

And if you were lucky enough to be in the house the next morning, you would've seen a young girl crying, holding a jar. A jar with a dead starfish in it. And a drowned spider. Both smiling in the way that only a dead starfish, or a dead spider, can.

To: Sandra J.
From: Iain S. Thomas
re: NEW BOOK! - Final Straw

No. You have misread my silence. We are not happy with the book. We cannot sell the animal stories, I can't think of a single publication that would buy them.

Iain, we are not a charity. There's no more money.

Things are going crazy here. We've booked media space for this book. We've made promises. I won't threaten you any more because right now, I'm begging you, write the real book.

People are going to lose their jobs over this and I hope you can sleep at night knowing that.

Kind Regards, Sandra

Iain S. Thomas @IWroteThisForU - Jun 14
There's nothing wrong with being shameless. The rest of us
are ruined.

To: Sandra J.
From: Iain S. Thomas
re: NEW BOOK! - Final Straw

Sandra.

This is all I've got left. There's no use asking for more because there isn't any. This was a mistake to begin with, a flash of light off the broken glass in my head that I mistook for an idea. We need to abandon this place before we all sink with it.

I'm telling you, I'm done. I've got nothing else.

- Iain

How To Be Happy. . .

For the last time.

This is all I've got.

Find the kind of person who, regardless of how bad things get, you can work it out with them. It doesn't matter what type of person they are when things are great, it matters how both of you respond when everything goes to hell.

I've been trying to write a book about how to be happy for forever now and I'm nowhere closer. I just keep starting and stopping and giving up and deleting everything and starting from scratch again. Sometimes I wake up in the middle of the night and I think to myself, I've got it!

But I really don't.

All I have is a feeling that the me tomorrow brings will be better than the me I'm stuck with today. But, as I already said somewhere, that's all you ever have. The you you are today.

I think I deleted that.

I try so hard to concentrate on the individual steps. It's all just a series of steps and nothing else matters. The people who walk with you will find their own roads, even those closest to you, and in the end, all you will have is each step you took.

If you are lucky, one day someone will come up to you on the road and take your hand and say, "It's time," and you'll shrug and both of you will climb a hill together and they will say to you, "Look how far you've walked," and you will look back out over the landscape and you will be amazed at how incredibly beautiful everything is.

None of that will matter unless you are happy in each and every step. The steps are all that ever matter. Don't look at the ground. Look up.

If I could reach out of these pages and hold your hand, I would. If I could make these words slide off the page and slowly ease themselves around you and hold you tight, if I knew how to do that, I would do it. Not for you but for me, because selfishly, I want to feel less alone.

This is a selfish book.

I desperately want to be happy. That's the truth. Maybe there is no happiness and all that exists is a kind of honesty you find in the universe, a moment of clarity between yourself and everything else where suddenly nothing and everything matters, and all of it's ok.

Maybe they're the same thing, honesty and happiness, as both of them can be so very rare.

Deep down, I know it is the bad things that happen to us that make us a story. Something bad happening to someone is the basis of every story ever written. How they respond to it is what we look for, because we're all just looking for tips on how to deal with the bad things that have happened to us.

What was the bad thing that happened to you?

What's your story?

I'm so sorry for whatever it was.

Here is the bad thing currently happening: Nothing bad, beyond my own morose, sad, obsession with myself, has actually happened in this story.

There is nothing more to write here.

Here are some things you can try at home.

- Go outside and think about what you've done.

- Make some kind of shake or a smoothie or something.

- I don't know.

July 2, 2014

To: Iain S. Thomas
From: Sandra J.
re: NEW BOOK! One last plea ...

Iain,

I've begged and the printers and the media company have given us one final extension. Am pulling every favour owed me. Please. Look at everything you've written, rinse it out and write the book I've promised everyone.

Your deadline to submit this manuscript to us has come and gone. We're supposed to be shooting a trailer for the book right now.

DO IT.

Kind Regards, Sandra

To: Sandra J.
From: Iain S. Thomas
re: NEW BOOK! One last plea ...

Sandra.

I can't promise anything because I don't think there's anything left.
I'm scraping the floor below the barrel.

Did you hear yet about the plane that got shot down over the
Ukraine today?

I can't believe all those people are dead. They were just going on
holiday or to a conference or whatever it was and now they're gone.
Death is just this sudden slice out of the black that takes you, and I
can't believe how the world is, how the world can do this to itself.
There were 215 kilograms of flowers on that plane.

The world is in an emergency and I've written an emergency poem
about it. Poems should be things behind glass that you can break
when bad things happen.

Please let people know the poem is available to them if they need it.

Keep well, Iain

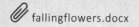
215 Kilograms Of Fresh Cut Flowers That Never Stop Falling

And maybe there was a kind god nearby
And he froze time for everyone onboard
And there are families who will forever be going on
And coming home from holidays
And there are people in business class
And they'll never disembark
And doctors are excited because they know the cure for
AIDS
And two dogs are on the greatest adventure of their lives
And all these toys falling from the sky will always belong
To happy children
And all these appointments will always be kept.

Iain S. Thomas @IWroteThisForU - Jul 17

We all become secrets when we die.

To: Iain S. Thomas
From: Sandra J.
re: NEW BOOK! - One last plea ...

You're right. The world is a horrible place.

And so is this book.

You've gone too far, Iain, and you don't seem to be coming back.

There will be consequences for this.

To: Sandra J.
From: Iain S. Thomas
re: NEW BOOK! - One last plea ...

Sandra.

My father died. He took all his secrets with him and that's the cruelest part of all. If I die in a car crash, when I am lying bleeding on the asphalt, I will take the one finger I can move and tap all my secrets in Morse code onto the ground, so that at least the ground knows who I was.

I kept trying to talk to him about something greater than where we were and what we were doing, about something bigger, something about all he'd done for us, about what I was going through, but I couldn't. He was tired. He saw me get married and maybe I should be thankful for that, if nothing else.

Did I ever tell you he couldn't read anything I wrote? His eyes were gone at the end. I wrote a #1 bestselling book and my own father couldn't read it. I think maybe my mother read bits of it to him but I wasn't there to explain it, to try and tell him what I was doing.

I haven't written anything besides these poems. They're not secrets. It's all I've got right now. Don't know when I'll be able to write anything about being happy.

My father's gone and now I am right up against the edge of time.

Now there's only everything he left behind.

- Iain

dad_1.docx

Dad,

Mom phoned and said
That you didn't wake up
And I'm sorry about that
My first instinct was to call you
And ask you what I should do
And tell you, I don't know why I should do anything
Any more
Because there's no one left to impress.

dad_2.docx

Dad,

Mom's ok
I wrote you a letter
And put it in the coffin
And it said "I'll take care of mom"
And I meant that.

dad_3.docx

Dad,

I touched your face one
Last time in the funeral home
And I've never touched anything
So cold in my life
And my first thought was
"At least you aren't suffering from the heat"
And you taught me to try and laugh at everything
That hurt
No matter what it was
Because that way it didn't hurt so much.

dad_4.docx

Dad,

It's been a while
But I still remember the way
Your brother turned away
At the funeral
As if there was somewhere to look
That didn't hurt.

dad_5.docx

Dad,

I grew a beard
So I see your face every now and again in the mirror
I haven't started talking to it yet but
Every time I fix a scratch on my car, I find another one
And I like to think you'd say
"Well that's life isn't it, might as well be happy"
Because that's the sort of stupid, warm, heartfelt thing
you'd just say.

To: Sandra J.
From: Iain S. Thomas
re: NEW BOOK! - More poetry

Sandra.

My father is still dead.

I'm not anywhere but I'm still writing to you, maybe because I know you won't respond. It's like talking to stars, their silence is what makes them such good listeners.

Did you know that today is the anniversary of the Marikana massacre? Here in South Africa, 44 miners were killed by the police in 2012 during a strike. They were lead by one man wearing a green blanket; 3000 men followed this one guy into a battle, a drill operator. The police shot him and he died.

I wrote this poem about what it felt like to see all the debate going on around me from people who'd never dug a hole, let alone worked in a mine, in their lives. I don't exclude myself from that.

Then I wrote a poem about a child begging at the traffic lights. There's also a longer poem about a gift passed down through a family for generations.

I don't write much about South Africa. I was born at the start of the 80s and if I was any more privileged, I'd be made of ivory and silver. I know that, perhaps, it's not my place to talk about these things and that the best thing I can probably do is keep quiet so other people's voices can be heard. But if I can't speak, I can write.

I know you're not interested.

I'm sending them anyway.

It's all attached.

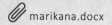

Mari-ka-na

I've never heard of it
But it's got the strange sound new words have
Like Osama Bin Laden
And you learn the way it sounds
So you can say it often
Because you know you'll need to
When everyone gets together
To solve the country's problems
From the comfort of our MacBooks

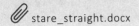

Stare Straight Ahead

I know you have problems, son
But today I'm staring straight ahead
I've been practicing my whole life
And soon I'll be able to see forever
Don't wash my windscreen
Don't try and tell me a joke
Don't juggle balls
Just don't
I'm perfecting staring straight ahead
One day, I'll be able to see the other side of you.

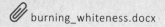

A Burning Whiteness

I have a gift for you my child.

It is a gift that's only ever taken.

Never given.

I will wrap it around you like a fire but know this:

Your clothes cannot hide it.

It will always be on your hands.

When they are open – when they are fists.

This gift will bond you to everyone else with the same gift, and you will help each other when things get hard, as we have done for hundreds of years.

Do not cry when life is hard, it will never be harder than our gift allows it to be.

You will never hear the sound of a window closing or a door locking as you cross the street.

You will never walk into a boardroom and have people wonder if you're only there because of some governmental decree.

Yes, sometimes, you will be in a car, or pulled into an office with other people with the same gift as you, and then you will all be expected to put your real cards on the table.

They will whisper and you will hear how they breathe.

You will be expected to let a mask fall to the floor, and let dark and honest air cool your real skin.

You will have special names for everyone who does not have the same special gift as you.

You will walk into a mall and the people doing the shopping will all look just like you.

You will watch movies and read books and the heroes will all look just like you.

You will join us as we tap away on our screens, using the words, "out of the bush," and making snide, thinly-veiled jokes that we can quickly point out are jokes.

Your gift allows you to say, "Can't you take a joke?"

Who could hate a joke?

Who could hate a gift?

You will never be casually told to "move on" from the most painful parts of your past.

No.

Your past will be remembered with gunfire at noon and somber moments of silence and statues.

This gift was your father's father's and his father's before him and he fought and killed and he took all he could before he died.

To give this gift to me.

To give this gift to you.

He did this for you.

You won't ever even have to think about what you have or where it comes from.

You will have the luxury of taking things for granted.

Of owning history and in turn, the future.

Of expecting these things to always be there, because they always have.

Of being owed an easy life.

People will talk of change.

You will have to say, "Yes, change is necessary."

But you will never actually have to change anything.

Not even your mind.

You will never have to use the superiority you might claim or your education to actually experience any kind of empathy for anyone else that doesn't share your gift.

It's not all roses.

Maybe you will worry about how you'll afford the rent in your home.

But you can always call me.

Or rely on the skills I have taught you.

This is the gift I have given you.

You must call out.

It will be too much of a shock if you are seen on the street with old, ragged clothes.

People will write articles and pass pictures of you around.

People will ask you what happened to you and point to you as, "An example of how bad things have really gotten."

We will hold you up like Jesus.

Children will say, "We saw Jesus at the traffic lights!"

If that upsets you, then protest.

When you do, you will never be considered a pawn of the government, a dumb thing, not even human, with no will of its own or nothing to say, nothing more than a manipulation, a distraction from the real issues of the day, which are so much more comfortable for all of us to discuss. Your gift gives you the right to choose what you want to discuss.

When you do, your protest will never be lumped together with the protest of others who look similar to you, you will never be expected to take responsibility for something done by someone else on the other side of the country who shares only the most basic of common denominators with you.

When you do, you will never have your protest dismissed as disgusting, as if protesting was something to be done politely and quietly, as if you'd done something unthinkable at a tea party you weren't invited to.

No.

When you protest, those around you will raise their cellphone cameras higher and higher and chant:

"THE WHOLE WORLD IS WATCHING.

THE WHOLE WORLD IS WATCHING."

And we will cry at the truly noble nature of your sacrifice and your protest, we will cry over you as we would cry over some fallen, noble bird.

We will cry as your white skin is broken like porcelain.

No.

Because this is your gift.

And it is taken.

Never given.

Perkins & Perkins & Associates

LAW & LEGAL ADVISORS - VANCOUVER - NEW YORK - LONDON - BANGKOK

12 September 2014

Mr. Iain S. Thomas

Dear Sir,

We act on behalf of Central Avenue Publishing on whose behalf we issue a final demand. In terms of your contract with our client you undertook to complete and deliver to them a manuscript by no later than 1 July. Despite numerous email requests on the part of our client and the passing of said date, you have failed to deliver the manuscript concerned. We also note with concern that our client's numerous attempts to contact you telephonically have been unsuccessful despite the leaving of numerous messages asking you to call them back.

We wish to point out that your failure to deliver the manuscript as provided for in the abovementioned agreement constitutes a breach of contract in respect of which you will be held liable for damages suffered by our client. In this regard we confirm that our client reserves its right to claim such damages.

Accordingly, we implore you to contact us at your earliest convenience.

For and on behalf of,

Perkins & Perkins

Iain S. Thomas @IWroteThisForU - Sep 13
Didn't make it to the shops on time, so I gave pieces of
myself away as gifts. Still trying to rebuild. Using a jar of
marmalade as a heart.

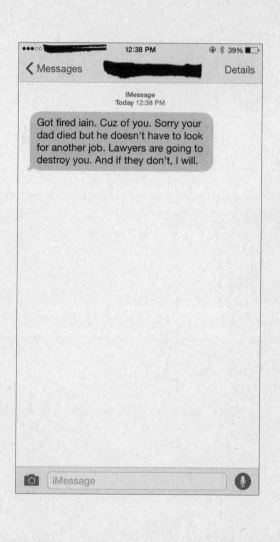

Iain S. Thomas @IWroteThisForU - Oct 12
"Sorry, just trying to get through," I said, destroying their lives forever.

To: customerservice@centralavenuepublishing.com
From: Iain S. Thomas
re: New Editor for Iain Thomas?

To Whom It May Concern:

Sorry.

Is anyone there?

Also, please advise if you'd be interested in a book about letters to superheroes.

See attached.

Iain S. Thomas

How To Be Happy?

Here is the bad thing that happened to me.

My father was diagnosed the year I was born. He got sick. What made him sick isn't really important so I'll just say, sick. Maybe you know someone who's sick too. The wires that criss-crossed his body started to short and fuse. Sometimes it was his hands. Sometimes it was his eyes. Eventually it was everything. I can remember him walking but only just. He was the kindest, gentlest man but also a man who refused to ever let anything, ever, get him down.

You could iron shirts on my father's stiff upper lip.

I remember once we walked past a restaurant, my father pushing himself along in his wheelchair, and a man sitting in front of an overflowing ashtray with a bouquet of flowers next to it saw us and he called me over.

"Give these to your father," he said.

He wanted me to give the flowers to my father because he thought they would mean something to him, that he was so terribly unhappy in the world, because he was sick, that he needed a stranger to give him flowers.

I gritted my teeth and said, "Ok," planning to just throw them in the bin as soon as he was out of view.

He said, "No, wait, call him over here. I want to see the smile on his face."

He thought my father was both physically, and mentally, disabled.

My father was the smartest man I ever met. He had a doctorate in foreign accounting. What I like to think I can do with words, he could do with numbers. I never understood it, but he did it, and it was important, and he was important.

That day, with the man and the flowers, was perhaps the closest I've ever come to killing a man; but I just walked away. I was 14 years old, and I never told my father about the man who wanted to give him flowers.

We would always smile in the face of everything. While that kind of positive attitude may sound like a good thing, it wasn't. I decided, somewhere along the line, that I could never, ever tell anyone how upset I really was. So I learned to control my emotions, completely, and never share them. I think entirely on the inside, never on the outside. I consider each and every single thing that comes out of my mouth. Because I can never let on that this is terrible. This is horrible.

I must smile.

Or at least, never let anyone know how I really feel. He died a short while after I got married and his body in the funeral home is the coldest thing I've ever touched. I have never loved a human being more than in the moment he was gone.

For this reason and others, I find it impossible to cheer at sporting events. I can never, and will never, let go.

Here is another memory: I would lie on the floor of the TV room and he would sit in his chair and I would have a blanket over me and I would rest my head on one of his feet. If that wasn't happiness, then it was at least a feeling of being safe and loved.

When we die, we leave behind echoes of who we were and his voice and the things he did and didn't do, the things he loved and the things he hated, they echo in me and everyone he ever interacted with. He echoes in me, constantly.

Here is something that is not a memory: Every morning, my wife and I play a brief bluffing game to see whose turn it is to make the coffee, we lie about who made it the day before and we both know we are lying. The person who loves the other just a little bit more that morning gives in and makes the coffee, and we watch the news together before the day begins. I am lucky because it happens every day, almost without fail.

My father only met my wife a few times but he liked her.

Now I don't even know what this is about any more. Now they'll sue me and ask for my advance back and we'll never be able to afford coffee ever again.

Here are some things you can try at home.

- Cry.

- Pick up things and put them down again.

- Stare out the window.

- Listen to people tell you that you look, "Tired."

- Feel tired. Look tired.

- Try to write.

- Fail.

Dear Professor X,

In the interests of being happy, I would like to apply for a position at your school for gifted children. While I do not have the ability to grow claws out my knuckles, shoot optic beams or control the weather, I do believe I have a particular skill set that may be of use on your team.

I can turn any women I date into a series of poems, prose and sometimes songs by the band known as the Counting Crows, over a period of one to two years. These women will also lose weight when we eventually break up. I first discovered this mutant ability in high school, when I began seriously dating a girl for the first time at the age of 16. Before this, I had simply kissed girls and neither the weight loss nor Counting Crows songs manifested, so I believe that an entire relationship is needed before my powers reach their zenith and maximum potential.

Slowly, while she was sleeping, I distilled her essence into a series of 4/5 line poems until I had captured all of who she was to me and the next phase of the process began – weight loss and resentment being the main characteristics of my strange, alien ability.

Over the years, I discovered that beyond Counting Crows, I could also turn girls into albums by Andrew Bird, Bob Dylan, Joy Division and once, even The Bangles, although that was a short-lived manifestation.

While I understand that you might be wondering how this could be of any use in a combative or strategic situation, I believe that were I to go into battle, I could find a female enemy with a penchant for a guy of a generally contemplative nature who writes occasionally depressing but vaguely optimistic poetry.

In finding the aforementioned enemy, I would be able to remove them from combat for a period of one to two years, before reducing them to thin husks of their former selves and the album, *August And Everything After*. This would be a surgical-strike style of relationship, with the power of a tactical nuke in terms of its impact on the battle. I would leave less emotional enemies to the likes of the other classmates at your school for the gifted. My power might not be an optic blast but man, when I take that girl out of the picture, she's gone.

There is, however, one caveat, I have met a girl who I cannot reduce to a bunch of songs, who refuses to lose weight as she's already in good shape, and resists my attempts to reduce her to poetry. I am happily dating this girl and will not be able to fight your enemies with my mutant abilities for the foreseeable future.

However, should you have a mutant who can travel back in time, and I believe you do, please find me between the ages of 16 and 31 and provide the past me with both this letter and your guidance in terms of how my powers might best be used to protect and serve mankind.

If you feel that my previous skill set could be of use to your institution please commence time travel immediately. I regret that I cannot help you now but I am too happy and happiness, unfortunately, destroys my Counting Crows-oriented abilities.

But *August And Everything After* is still a good album.

Best regards, Iain

Here at last, we shall be free.

How No One Buries Someone

In Uncategorized on December 10, 2014 at 3:49am

When they knew someone was dying
they called each person who had ever loved someone
and told them to come to someone's side
and that whatever they'd taken from someone
they should return
and each put something next to someone's bed

a lock of hair
a box of matches
a note
a shard of glass
an old book
a mixtape
an empty bottle
and so when someone died

no one had anything left that belonged to someone else
and no one was sad

at all.

<34 comments>

To: customerservice@centralavenuepublishing.com
From: Iain S. Thomas
re: New Editor for Iain Thomas?

To Whom It May Concern:

I don't know if you're getting these mails, but here is something I wrote in response to the Charlie Hebdo shootings and all the hate I saw on my Facebook wall afterwards.

Could you sell it to one of the news agencies?

Does CNN buy poetry?

Please advise.

- Iain S. Thomas

P.S. I've also written a poem for NASA called "We Will Never Leave Earth." Please let them know they can stop working now.

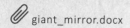

A Giant Mirror In The Desert

Now's the time to hate who you want to hate.

We can hate the people who killed people.

We can hate the people who provoked the people who killed people.

We can hate the injustice of it all.

We can hate the people who say, "They had it coming" and we can hate the people who say, "It doesn't sound like you have much faith in your religion if it can be toppled by a cartoon."

We can hate the media for circling it for days like vultures circling a rotting carcass.

We can hate the media who don't cover the things we want them to cover.

We can all hate everyone we need to hate for a while.

We can hate the moderates, the politically-correct and the apologists who allowed this to happen.

We can hate the extremists and the die-hards and the people who refuse to see anything differently.

We can hate the people who are trying to make it about something other than what it is.

We can hate the people who are for the guns that killed people.

We can hate the people who are against the guns those who died could've protected themselves with.

We can hate those who find hate as an answer before we've even asked the question.

"What are you in high school, you fucking jerk-off, go write another poem, you faggot, or put your fucking boots on and learn to hate."

Because hate is comfortable, like an old chair you know and love.

You can put hate on like a pair of Levi's you've had forever.

"What kind of pussy are you for not hating someone at a time like this?"

Hate like a river that flows to many fields.

Hate like a flower that blooms in your heart.

"Let's bomb the fucking desert into glass and make a mirror so big you could hold it up to God's face and scream,

Look at what you've done.

Look at what you've done."

And if we hate enough and we're lucky, he'll send an angel to tell us who was right.

But it was you.

You were always right.

He'll say each of us is a universe.

He will lean down and take your face in his hands and whisper it again and again.

"It was always you.

You were always right."

My child, you will weep, for all the hate, you love.

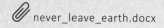

We Will Never Leave Earth

Battlestar Galactica, is a lie.

Star Trek, is a lie.

Alien, is a lie.

We will never leave Earth.

We will never leave Earth because we will spend the time we have left and the one chance we have to leave Earth bickering over who did what to who.

We will never leave Earth because instead of building spaceships, we decided to build walls and razor wire and prisons and bombs.

We will never leave Earth because we aren't building space elevators and warp drives and new kinds of space suits and lasers - just in case we ever meet anyone as petty and mean as ourselves out there.

We will never leave Earth because we're too busy building tanks to fight over the last barrels of oil and planes to drop the bombs we made on the people who disagree with us over the specifics of the story about where we all come from.

We will never leave Earth, even though all our stories agree, that heaven is above us.

We will never leave Earth. Even though Stephen Hawking says we've only got 200 years left. The last 2000 don't give us much hope.

We will never leave Earth because so many of us have agreed that passing laws about what someone else does with their genitals is more important than leaving the Earth.

We will never leave Earth and we will sink and drown on this ship while we fight over the deck chairs.

We will never leave Earth.

The Last Starfighter, is a lie.

Babylon 5, is a lie.

Star Wars, is a lie.

Iain M. Banks, is a lie.

We will, never, leave Earth.

We will never leave Earth and we will never be anything more than a strange thought the universe had, a moment in which it went, "Heh, wouldn't that be crazy. Na."

We will never leave Earth because the world will erupt in fire and ice while we're still debating whether or not fire and ice actually exist. We will still be arguing over whether we're burning or freezing to death when we die.

We will never leave Earth and the few robots we've sent out in our place will be our only fingerprints on the firmament, the only proof that a grabbing, desperate hand shot out of our coffin, before it sunk beneath the soil.

We will never leave the Earth and meet Aries, Taurus, Gemini, Cancer, Leo, Virgo, Libra, Scorpio, Sagittarius, Capricorn, Aquarius, or Pisces.

We will never touch Gemini's face and hear her say, "You look just like me. You look just like me."

We will never leave Earth because we're too busy arguing over who you're allowed to love to bother actually doing the work of love, of leaving the Earth.

We will never leave the Earth because we're obsessed with the soil we were born on and we never realised that all the dirt that we stand on and all the dirt we're made of, isn't dirt. It's star dust. Our dirt, is their dirt, and we will never ask their dirt for help and so, we will never leave Earth.

Carl Sagan, is a lie.

Douglas Adams, is a lie.

Guardians of the Galaxy, is a lie.

Space Quest, is a lie.

We will, never, leave Earth.

Except as dust and ashes and minerals, returned to the sender, to be light, burning, in someone else's stars.

Iain S. Thomas @IWroteThisForU · Jan 11
The worst part about growing older is watching your
friends become the people you hated when you were
young.

Here at last, we shall be free.

Still, Quiet

In Uncategorized on January 12, 2015 at 7:48am

Even though my heart is quiet now,
I still listen to it.
I do not listen to my head.
All it does is provide commentary while I do the things,
I did not know I would do.
I do not listen.

I still listen to the quiet in my heart.

<75 Comments>

Here at last, we shall be free.

WHO?   FOLLOW ME - I'M GOING TO GET CANDY   BUY SOME BOOKS   ARCHIVES   RSS FEED

On A Personal Note

In Uncategorized on January 15, 2015 at 9:36am

I've tried to tell them it just needs an ending but I can't get anyone on the phone and they don't respond to my emails. Maybe I've bankrupted them. I think they just feel angry and sorry for me. And that they're going to sue me, despite how sorry they feel for me.

Someone asked how the book was going on the phone the other day and I almost screamed, "FINE!" but I just said, "fine," instead, because that's what I do.

In my mind, there are people, still standing at printers, missing their families, staring at watches, waiting for someone to run into the room with thumb-drive and yell, "Fire it up boys, we've got the ultimate goddamn secret to happiness."

<125 Comments>

Iain S. Thomas @IWroteThisForU - Jan 16
Hopelessness is learned.

Iain S. Thomas @IWroteThisForU - Jan 16
What I mean is we are taught to be cynical by millions of
little failures, desperate and otherwise. You have to unlearn
it all somehow.

Iain S. Thomas @IWroteThisForU - Jan 16
Otherwise, you are just what you're left with.

Here at last, we shall be free.

800 Secret Prayers In Tuam

In Uncategorized on January 21, 2015 at 2:02pm

They found the bodies of 800 babies
In a septic tank at an Irish home for unwed mothers
Their only gravestone was
A news story in the Washington Post
No word on whether or not
A fog of last breaths
Lit the air each morning
Seeping out of the wet ground
Something read over morning coffee
And I cannot help but think
I said the words "starlit distant ocean"
In a memorial poem for my wife's mother
And I said the words "How dare you pity this man?"
In my father's eulogy
And I said a thousand, thousand things about other things
But I would struggle to say the 800 words that each one
Must have had
As a name.

<34 comments>

Iain S. Thomas @IWroteThisForU - Jan 22
There we all were, trying to be better people than we could
ever hope to be.

Here at last, we shall be free.

Write A Shit Poem If It Makes You Happy

In Uncategorized on February 1, 2015 at 12:34am

It's fine.
Maybe you can make it ironic.
Something that feels like a girl in a short skirt at a party.
Offending her sensibilities with her own humour.
Daring you to love her and playing never-to-get.
Pretend there's a joke that only her and the people who like the
poem know.
Wink.

Maybe you can make it angry.
And tell a story of how strong your mother was.
She raised you all on her own.
Or how drunk your father was.
Act like you were born on railroad tracks.
Maybe your father was a train.
Get someone to play an 808 in the background.

Maybe you can put it in the middle of the road.
Pontificate a little.
Become a vanilla paste of words.
Don't say anything really.
Wonder about the nature of a pen.
Be clever.

Maybe you can make it impenetrable.
Be as vague as possible.

Slam your fist into a grapefruit and make a kind of growling noise.
Roll your eyes as soon as someone asks you what it means.
Snap your fingers to show you don't understand.
Wear a beret.

Maybe you can make it a history lesson.
Talk about the plants and leaves that grew around you.
Tell me something about a smell you remember from a kitchen.
Shock me with some kind brutality either inflicted or received or witnessed.
Write one of the words in a language I don't understand.
Put it in italics.

Maybe you can make it real sensitive.
Write words that kiss the skin.
Make them sound like the space between two drum beats.
Talk about what it feels like to breathe.
Or something.

Who cares.
Because poetry is the only art form that people naturally expect to be,
shit.

So it's ok to write shit poetry.

It's fine.

< 7 comments>

Iain S. Thomas @IWroteThisForU - Feb 11
We are only who we really are when we're completely
alone.

20 Things You Won't Believe This Poem Did Next

In Uncategorized on February 12, 2015 at 11:11am

You will not lose weight with this one weird old tip.
You will not meet singles in your area.
A little girl with cancer was not saved by an injection of the HIV/
AIDS virus.
Beyonce is not fucking the president.
Other people do not hate him.
You will not win a free iPad.
You are not the one millionth viewer of this website.
None of these 12 movies that were nearly made would've been good.
Your computer is not running slow.
You can't make this much money from home.
15 minutes is not all you need.
What's on your mind isn't worth posting.
No one is giving away free watches.
You will need your credit card.
This will not improve your life, right now.
This is not something you can do today to make people like you.
There is no miracle food.
Stop looking at pictures of fat celebrities.
The world is beautiful but the people who live in it will lie to you.
Live with truth and meaning and don't be distracted by anything
else.

<3 comments>

Here at last, we shall be free.

WHO?   FOLLOW ME - I'M GOING TO GET CANDY   BUY SOME BOOKS   ARCHIVES   RSS FEED

Write About Something Else

In Uncategorized on February 13, 2015 at 12:59am

Write about something that makes you feel uncomfortable.

Write about something that makes you worry what other people will think.

Write with black ink on a white page in a quiet room, so you can hear the nib tattooing the paper.

Write with your headphones on, bashing away at the keyboard, angrily.

Write in the speech bubbles that come off a comic book character's head.

Write a short play about the inner turmoil that dominated your misspent youth.

Write a violent critique of a self-indulgent play about the inner turmoil that dominated a misspent youth.

Write to try and sound like Hemingway, Saul Williams, Bukowski, ee cummings, Adam Duritz, Rumi, Alan Watts or someone else.

Write to try and capture your own unique voice and take on things.

And if one day, there's nothing left to write about, then that's the exciting part.

Because the need to write, will remain, and that's when you'll finally write

Something new.

\<2 comments\>

Here at last, we shall be free.

Do It Anyway

In Uncategorized on February 14, 2015 at 6:13pm

Maybe one day you'll wake up and you'll find
That you can't even give your art
Away
That so many people have made art
That there's too much
And no one has time to sift through the junk
To find your pictures.
But make art, anyway.
Maybe one day you'll get to your first gig
And the only people there will be
Your family
And they'll be the only ones clapping
When you're done
And everyone else at the bar, they just
Go back to their drinks.
But make music, anyway.
Maybe one day you'll write the most moving thing
Ever written, and if anyone ever read it
They'd cry
If they ever found it amongst the one thousand
Thousand, thousand, thousand
Other things that have been written
Like bills and tax returns.
But write beautiful things, anyway.
Because even if the only person you impress at the end is you
It will be
Worth
It.
<2 comments>

Iain S. Thomas @IWroteThisForU - Feb 15
To the things we devour and the things that devour us.

To: customerservice@centralavenuepublishing.com
From: Iain S. Thomas
re: Is Anyone There?

To Whom It May Concern at Central Avenue Publishing,

Attached is the rest of my book. I understand Sandra doesn't work there any more, please show this to whoever has replaced her. Maybe they'll know what I'm talking about.

Iain S. Thomas

How To Be.

Here I am in the dark. Unprepared and alone.

Where is happiness, in the dark?

Everything here feels rehearsed and fake, no matter what I do. Like I've been practicing looking nonchalant in a mirror before taking a picture.

How can I make something real in the dark? I wish I was like blinds on a window and I could decide how much light to let in, I would flood my heart with light right now if I could. But I can't.

There you are, thinking, "He should've just stuck to that poetry blog. Honey, come over here and watch, you know the poetry guy? He's narrating his nervous breakdown as it happens."

Here I am in the dark and you are watching behind a glass window while I commit career suicide over what was supposed to be an easy book to write.

Are you happy now?

There's no more politeness, even terse politeness, no communication at all. It's all gone. Only desperation and frustration remain.

Any minute now, there'll be a knock on the door and they'll take away my keyboard, my coffee maker and my car and my TV and everything else. We'll stay with friends or maybe our cousins. There's no one else left.

I'm sorry, I've done little else but fail you repeatedly.

Just for the record, I was going to write a book called, '300 Things I Hope,' because I need hope and maybe other people do too, maybe even more than happiness, but there's none now. I will just say the things I was going to say in that book to the squirrels in the park. If they'll have my wife and me. If we end up staying in a park.

In the end, this is all I know:

Who you are is a coin hidden underneath a sheet of paper. You have to take life like a pencil and rub it against the paper to see who you are, to find the bumps and lines.

The more hard, difficult things you go through, the more you know who you are and the clearer the picture of you becomes.

I know who I am, and on a good day, how to be me.

I don't know how to be happy even if sometimes, as if by accident, I am.

Maybe knowing who you are, can be enough.

Here are some things you can try at home.

- Just try to be ok.

Dad,

In Uncategorized on March 1, 2015 at 3:28am

It's the future
But we haven't worked out a way to move ourselves out of our
bodies
So I'm still a little sad
I'm going to listen to everyone patiently today
And be kind and gentle and wise when they're quiet
And make people smile every chance I get
And try to be stronger than I am
I still don't know how you sat at the back door
And looked out at the backyard like it was endless
How you'd love the three of us
In the different ways we needed to be loved
I just remember how you'd sit in the light in a comfortable silence
I don't remember all the jokes but that's ok
I still remember how you'd laugh
And what that sounded like
I'll take the roof off the car later
And drive somewhere nice
You've been gone a while now
But I'm going to spend today with you
I'll be a better, stronger man tomorrow
Just not today

<1 comments>

Here at last, we shall be free.

WHO?   FOLLOW ME - I'M GOING TO GET CANDY   BUY SOME BOOKS   ARCHIVES   RSS FEED

A Tiny Hole In The Heart

In Uncategorized on March 3, 2015 at 2:15pm

You just take the human heart and you click back the cover.

Underneath the cover, next to the battery is a tiny hole the size of the universe.

You take a paperclip and you straighten it out, like someone you love would help straighten you out.

You push it through your soul first and remember that you're piercing it to remind yourself to feel.

Then you push the paperclip into the tiny hole the size of the universe.

You wait until all the stars blink three times.

You keep holding it all in and holding it all down until you hear a beep.

And that's how you reset the human heart.

<0 comments>

Here at last, we shall be free.

WHO?   FOLLOW ME - I'M GOING TO GET CANDY   BUY SOME BOOKS   ARCHIVES   RSS FEED

I Know Why People Are Like They Are

In Uncategorized on March 15, 2015 at 4:56pm

I know now why people are like they are because I've been given enough time to be some of them by now.

I think you miss everyone eventually. I think it's demeaning to miss the kid who spat on my school uniform or the other kids who laughed and I thought I'd hate them forever but I don't, I just miss everyone.

You grow up and you want more and more and more from the hosepipe and it gives you all you can drink if you hold it right and then one day you're done and you say, 'stop,' and it doesn't, and you find yourself trying to hold water in your hands, and it runs down your wrists.

I'm petrified there's a kind of nostalgia that freezes you in place and makes you (me) forget that you'll (I'll) miss this too one day.

Isn't that the truth? You can't miss something until it's taken away? How do you ever know what'll go next and isn't it unfair that you can't hold everything to your chest all at once?

Sometimes I will walk into a room surrounded by so much history that I am overwhelmed and I don't know if everyone gets that or if it's just me but I know for sure these days, I am no fun at parties any more.

<0 comments>

To: Iain S. Thomas

From: michelle@centralavenuepublishing.com

re: Change of Editors - CAP

Hi Iain,

Please allow me to introduce myself. I'm Michelle, I've taken over Sandra's authors and will be managing your relationship with the company from now on.

I've gone through the email chain you've had with her and I have to say on behalf of the company, I'm incredibly sorry. She's completely misrepresented us. She had some kind of psychotic break by the looks of things.

I'm afraid to inform you that she shot one of her other authors with a BB gun. He's fine, she just winged him. Of concern to you is that a large collage of web images downloaded from social media sites of your work was found in her home. It was almost a kind of homage to you and your work – you know, all stuck to a wall with candles and incense burning underneath? I heard a rumour that she had one of those bobble-head type dolls with a bunch of pins stuck in its head. I don't think it was meant to be you, though. I don't think so anyway.

Also, there is no law firm called Perkins & Perkins. She sent that herself.

To be honest, none of us even knew you were busy with a new book, the 'advance' she sent you was a royalty check we owed you.

Finally, I think we might be able to do something with what you've sent us, if you'll continue to have us? Attached please find a new contract and advance (plus interest and an amount for damages) for the new book.

So you can hang on to the TV, your coffee maker and your keyboard.

Most sincerely,

Michelle

To: michelle@centralavenuepublishing.com
From: Iain S. Thomas
re: Change of Editors - CAP

Hi Michelle,

This is all a bit of a shock to me. I'm not quite sure what to say.

I think I'd like to make some changes.

Maybe the whole bit about how happiness will cause World War III is a bit much.

Maybe the story about how the scarecrow lost his heart is too dark.

Maybe I should be ok with using the letter 'e' in the book.

Maybe it shouldn't contain different pictures of my pen collection.

Let's take out the part where I die in the middle and the part where I die at the start.

Maybe the whole book shouldn't be set in italics, only some bits.

I think we should take most of that out.

Also, I don't want to repeat my mistakes but, would you be interested in a book about the internet but written like it was The Bible? I started writing in the middle of the night because I wasn't sure what else to do.

Please advise (and thank you),

Iain

THE BOOK OF THE INTERNET

Chapter 1.

In in the beginning, in the town of Los Angeles, 1994.

It came to be in the town of Los Angeles that an Oracle did descend from the heavens and approach me one night as I lay slumbering.

And it roused me with its pulsating light that did turn the insides of my eyes a dull red colour that slowly faded back to black, again and again.

And it said to me, "Awake, sir, for I am here to bestow upon you a mighty gift and indeed, a gift for all mankind."

I did sit up straight and heed the Oracle's words.

"I can answer any question you have. I am the complete sum of human intelligence throughout history. And if the answer does not exist yet, millions of people could be thinking about it in seconds, all you need to do is ask the question. I am the greatest, most sublime phenomenon since the invention of language itself and I am here for you, whenever you need me. What would you like to know? What would you like to see? Who would you like to listen to? What will be the first request you ask of the Oracle?"

And I did say unto the Oracle, "I would like to look at a naked woman. But after that, I'd like to read some poetry."

Her eyes did glow, as her blouse slipped to the floor, and walked towards me.

She whispered, "Everything must end. Especially a book about being happy."

As she took my hand, I asked her why anything had to end, ever.

She never replied.

Here at last, we shall be free.

WHO?   FOLLOW ME - I'M GOING TO GET CANDY   BUY SOME BOOKS   ARCHIVES   RSS FEED

The man who would not die

In Uncategorized on March 31, 2015 at 1:00pm

no matter how much they tried to get him in the coffin

they called for help and the entire world came

to help push down the lid

and put him in the ground

like ants on food

him at the bottom

still knocking on wood

<368 comments>

IAIN S. THOMAS IS A NEW MEDIA ARTIST AND AUTHOR. AS AN AUTHOR, HIS MOST FAMOUS WORK IS *I WROTE THIS FOR YOU*, WHICH HE WRITES UNDER THE PSEUDONYM 'PLEASEFINDTHIS' - A BLOG THEN BOOK THAT'S BEEN ON BOTH THE AMAZON AND iTUNES POETRY BESTSELLER LISTS SINCE ITS LAUNCH IN DECEMBER 2011.

HE REGULARLY WRITES FOR THE HUFFINGTON POST ON POETRY, CREATIVITY AND LIFE.

IAIN CURRENTLY LIVES IN CAPE TOWN, SOUTH AFRICA.

Also By Iain S. Thomas

I Wrote This For You

I Wrote This For You: Just the Words

I Wrote This For You and Only You

Intentional Dissonance

25 Love Poems for the NSA